Lady With Chains

Roch Carrier

LADY WITH CHAINS

Translated by Sheila Fischman

Anansi

Toronto   Buffalo   London   Sydney

Originally published in French as *La dame qui avait des chaînes aux chevilles*. Copyright © Editions internationales Alain Stanké Ltée., 1981.

Cover design: Laurel Angeloff

Translated with assistance from the Canada Council. Published with assistance from the Canada Council and the Ontario Arts Council, and manufactured in Canada for

House of Anansi Press Limited
35 Britain Street
Toronto, Ontario M5A 1R7
Canada

Canadian Cataloguing in Publication Data

Carrier, Roch, 1937 —
   [La dame qui avait des chaînes aux chevilles, English]
   Lady with chains

   (Anansi fiction series ; AF 47)
   Translation of: La dame qui avait des chaînes aux chevilles.
   ISBN 0-88784-139-2

   I. Title.   II. Title: La dame qui avait des chaînes
aux chevilles. English.   III. Series.

   PS8505.A77D3513 1984   C843'.54   C84-098217-8
   PQ3919.2.C25D313 1984

1 2 3 4 5 / 90 89 88 87 86 85 84

Roch Carrier photo: Pierre Gaudard
Sheila Fischman photo: Don Winkler

After the bevel had broken the nut that held the iron ring fast about her ankle, the chain dropped from her foot, which was close by the anvil. First, the Lady saw the burn that encircled her ankle. The chain now lying on the cobblestones no longer made the echoing lament that had for so long accompanied her in the prison. How long had she lived there, how many years? She watched her foot glide slowly along the cobblestones. It no longer dragged that cold resounding weight. Was this unconstrained foot hers? It was so light. She couldn't feel it as it rested on the ground. Beneath her foot, now free, the ground scarcely existed. Ahead of her, the ship's masts swayed against the sky. Men were rushing about. Boxes swung from cables. Nets lifted lowing animals into the air. Some people embraced, while others waved from the ship. The Lady could do nothing but look at her foot without its chain, her foot now free beneath her torn and muddy cotton skirt. Trying to walk, she collapsed.

Unfettered now, her legs no longer supported her. She was free, she could not move forward. She didn't even wonder if she had scraped her hands on the cobblestones. In her chains, she had fallen so often that she'd forgotten pain. She had been in chains for so long. Now that she was free, she couldn't run away. Why run away, if she was free? They could always recapture the Lady, close the iron ring about her ankles once again, hammer it shut on the anvil, then lead her back to prison, after a long journey in a cart along a broken road. When the horses no longer had the strength to pull the cart that was crammed with girls, when they no longer obeyed either threats or blows, the soldiers would whip the girls, who would then throw themselves on the ground; the soldiers would hit them again with their rifle butts to make them move on, their bare feet weighed down by chains that caught on pebbles and bumps. At night when the soldiers were even drunker, they would grunt at the girls huddling in the grass, then lift their skirts, spread their legs and finally fall asleep, choking with laughter. The Lady was free. She would not return to prison, she wouldn't take another dreadful journey in which nightmares weren't part of sleep but part of life, she would no longer be jostled about in a cell, tossed onto straw where she would shiver as if the sun had been extinguished. Now her feet were free, and she wanted to run to the ship and board it. The ship was already moving with the motion of the sea. She could not walk. She had stared too long at stone walls as motionless as sorrow, she couldn't believe she was seeing the ship with its swaying masts. She wanted to jump on the boat before she was dragged back to prison. The straw in her dungeon cell was never changed. She had forgotten that wet straw can be replaced by dry straw that creaks and still holds some sun and the smell of the fields. She didn't want to go back to that wet straw from which she had sometimes been driven away by rats. She shivered. The ship with its bobbing masts seemed to be heading out to sea. The Lady couldn't move along the cobblestones. She was going to return to her solitary cell, to the straw that was so cold. Never would she board the ship bound for a country where she would live without chains at her ankles or rotten straw underneath her body. Her legs no longer held her up. She would be put in prison again. Now she could only crawl. In her ribs, a rifle butt. A familiar shock. She did not start. Such blows weren't unusual. She would never reach the outbound ship. The Lady's body was shaken by grief as if the child she had once been was suddenly shuddering inside her woman's body. Once more, the rifle butt. This time it hurt. She was being lifted up so they could put her in chains again, then pushed into the cart that would take her back to the dungeon where no ray of sun ever penetrated. She felt cold, as if the door of her dungeon cell had suddenly opened before her. Hands were pushing her. A voice was saying something behind her shoulder. The voice wasn't shouting or roaring. The Lady didn't hear.

"Poor wretched child."

Hands were pushing her. She was going to end up back in the cell. The stone was always weeping icy tears that would soak the straw of her damp mattress. Rats would poke about in it. Sometimes they would bite her legs, at other times her face. They had also gnawed at her skirt. She had never got used to the rotten straw as she had to the blows, to the shouting and hunger. During the first days she was racked by hunger; now, it scarcely touched her. Her burns had faded. She no longer even wanted to eat. When they brought her bowl, the great wooden door with iron corners slammed against the wall. The sound always reminded her of the thunderstorms of her childhood. Then she would lap up her soup like a dog. And once more the prods, once more the hands pushing her. Had they put chains on her ankles again? Had they closed the iron ring? She was being taken back to prison. Had the ship and its swaying masts, the yards and the rigging, been only a dream?

The voice the Lady thought she'd heard, that hadn't shouted or spat insults, was a voice she'd never heard before.

"Poor wretched child, she must be so cold!"

Surely her dream was deceiving her. The thought of life outside this dungeon, which must be quite unlike the stagnant life lived there amid rotting straw, made her almost delirious. Her thoughts weren't attached to her body, they weren't tethered to the straw, they weren't held back by the chain, they weren't shut in behind cemented stones whose joints resisted fingernails, resisted the old stone she'd picked up that was more precious than a purse filled with gold; her thoughts could pass through the door reinforced with intertwined iron fitments; her thoughts could flee this smell where time rotted like a forgotten fruit. Often the Lady accompanied her thoughts and passed through the cemented stone walls; most likely she had followed her reverie all the way to the ship that was breathing the fresh sea air. She had thought it would take her to the other side of the sea so that never again would she see the eternal night of the solitary cell where time and life lay rotting! She had thought she'd progress through the great winds that would erase those days and nights that clung to her skin like the spoiled peel of a fruit. She had thought that glittering light as bright as the sea would give her heart the desire to be carried away, that it would make her thoughts as light as a bird that can soar and never collide against a vault of sweating stones. She had thought she would be able to drift away with her thoughts, free as a dream. And yet, the voice that she had heard, that wasn't shouting . . . It could only be human. Was it as false as the image of rigging and masts? The voice was saying:

"Poor child, she must be so cold . . . Put a cloak over her shoulders."

She didn't feel cold now, she had learned not to be cold. She was only unhappy. The cloak that covered her must have been invented by her thoughts to save her from the wet straw in her solitary cell. Yet her body was warm; it was covered with a breath as warm as wool. She had forgotten wool, but her body was as warm as though it were wrapped in it. The cloak, if it wasn't a dream, would have been wool. The light was so bright it could burn your eyes, but after so many days without hope, she couldn't believe in the light. Were the masts swaying, or her body? She knew she was being pushed toward her cell even though her feet, under the heavy wool cloak, free of chains, were advancing along the gangway; no hands were pushing at her back now, no rifles were pounding at her ribs. Set free now, she walked, her body enclosed in warmth that was like a sound sleep.

"This way, little lady! Come."

The new voice hadn't shouted. It hadn't reviled her. Two hands were held out to her. Hands that didn't want to strike her.

"Don't be afraid, little lady, the boat's strong enough to carry you. Even I, though I'm not a boat, I could carry you in my arms," said the soldier who was not inflamed by alcohol.

The voice was laughing now. She turned around, looked at the sky, at the harbor, at the houses all squeezed together, the crates, the heaps of bundles, the penned animals, the people who were rushing and bustling, calling and gesturing. She knew that she was dreaming, that soon she would awaken and find herself back on the damp straw, in the dungeon cell whose vault seemed to be constantly pressing upon her. One day it would crush her. She was dreaming. If she had opened her eyes she would have noticed the cart, the girls in chains, the soldiers. Where was she? She had lost her way, without chains, in a dream. Already her body was becoming too heavy for her legs. The dream was too great for her eyes. She faltered. Before she crashed down on the bridge of the ship, the soldier took into his arms the Lady with the rich woman's cloak and the poor woman's face. Her beauty was hidden by pain.

"Don't get sick right away, little lady! Wait till we're out to sea!"

She had heard. The tall masts and the many riggings weren't a dream. She left her country, she left her dungeon cell.

*   *   *   *   *

"I still see you, Virginie, your eyes lost in a story you aren't telling me. Ah, Virginie! You dream and you dream, as if that's all life was about. You're going to get lost in your daydreams, Virginie. You'll lose your way and never find us again. Even now you aren't with us. Is it the winter that's making you ill? When you look around the cabin the snow seems like a great troubled sea, but we're not adrift, Virginie. There's a cabin around us that drives the wind away. There's a fire in the cabin, there's wild hare to eat, I have a rifle; don't be afraid, Virginie, even though the wind is moaning like a dead soul. Spring will return, Virginie, and put an end to your suffering from this cold that burns your feet and fingers. Spring's very close, Virginie, it's already hiding in some of the trees: I've seen buds at the tips of frozen branches, Virginie. March is nearly over. It will be April soon. Spring will drive the snow away, Virginie. Winter will be forgotten, like something that never existed. You'll see how beautiful the land is hereabouts. There's plenty of stones, but the two of us, we'll pick them up and we'll be left with fine clear earth. And I'll sow seeds, Virginie. We'll have our first harvest, our first wheat, our first vegetables; don't be sad, Virginie. I'll go on felling trees: our estate will grow. I'll build a lean-to on our cabin: I want an ox, Virginie, and you can gather wildflowers and transplant them in front of the cabin. Soon it will look like a proper house: flowers all around, vegetables in the garden, fields in back of the house. Starting this summer, Virginie, we'll be proper bourgeois! Don't let the winter freeze your heart. Life will be beautiful again, Virginie. Christ had to die on the cross so He could rise from the dead on Easter morning; and we must get through the winter if we're to see the blossoms of spring. When spring comes, everything will start again. Our life's been rough, Virginie, but we're on our way to a springtime more beautiful than we've ever seen. We have land, Virginie. It's ours, yours and mine . . . You're my soul, Virginie, and I'm your body. And you know that the soul mustn't run away from the body. In the spring, Virginie, your sadness will melt like ice. You mustn't stray into daydreams and lose your way before spring. The soul must live with the body; you're my soul, Virginie. Think about the true springtime. Don't get lost in your thoughts, Virginie; I know that they're deeper and colder than snow. You know how a person can lose his way in the snow. I know that too, Virginie . . ."

Virginie knows how to kill that man. She will kill him. That man has caused death. She will be the cause of his. All men and women wear about their ankles the chains of life and of death. She will go to prison, enchained like the Lady, but she will kill that man. She no longer speaks to him, no longer looks at him, no longer listens to him. He is already dead. When spring is over, this summer, she will kill him. When he's not hunting the rifle is propped up in the corner by the door. She has never touched the rifle, even though that man has been rightly sentenced to death. A woman must not kill a man with a rifle. "Silence is death, Virginie. Winter has no voice: winter is silence. For days and days now, Virginie, you've known only silence. As long as we've been in this cabin you've been as silent as ice. But when I look in your eyes, Virginie, I see sad shadows passing. Too much silence means that death is prowling around. Is death prowling around you, Virginie? You and me, we've seen death. But you mustn't cling to death: hold it back, don't let it go on its way. Don't keep it in your head, Virginie, let it pass. It has wrapped us in a dark blizzard, Virginie. But the wind's died down now. Don't let it stay in your thoughts. We'll start our lives over, at the point when death struck us. We can begin with the spring that will soon be here. Spring's like giving birth, Virginie; the heart of life begins to beat again. And it's life you must choose. Silence isn't life. If a nest in a tree is filled with silence, there's no life in that nest. If there's silence in a river, that river's turned to ice. Virginie, don't leave your heart in the ice. If you wanted, you could bring the springtime into our cabin now, today, under our roof that's hunchbacked under the snow. Say one word to me, Virginie, just one, and I promise you that life will begin again; say just one word and your sorrow will melt like the snow in April."

That man talks on and on but she will keep silent. She will speak to him only when she brings about his death. She knows how to avoid talking to a man. She knows how to kill a man. She won't touch the rifle. If she could she'd forbid him even to listen to her breathing. He doesn't deserve to have in his presence a woman who draws breath. That man must be punished. He must be punished with silence and death. She will wait for the coming of summer, she will wait with the patience of death which sometimes torments its victim for a long time. She could choose not to kill, she could simply go away, toss a few clothes into a bag, a few loaves of bread, a chunk of frozen meat, and leave this cabin and walk, walk, back to where she came from, or run away to some other place, and then that man would be only memories of snow and swirling wind. But these memories cannot be forgotten; they are carved too deeply in her flesh, they have left a frostbite that nothing, ever, no forgetting, will ever warm. She is doomed, then, to live in the same cabin with him, to warm her hands at the same stove, to hang her clothes on the same wall; she is forced to sleep in the same bed, upon the same spruce boughs; every day she must eat meat that he has hunted; she cannot run away from him like someone waking from a nightmare. She will stay with him and she will kill him. Henceforth that man is a stranger: he has done what no man she has ever known would be capable of doing. She knows how to kill a man and that man will die. He talks on and on as if he were going to live for centuries. He fills the cabin with words, as if words were important to one who is going to die. Does he think his words will keep death from entering the cabin? Only God knows the time and place where a human creature will fall asleep forever, in death. She shares this secret with God. She does not listen to that man as he talks, but she knows in what season his belly will be too small for the pain that will burn it. That man talks as if he were going to live forever. At the end of their long walk through this forest that resembles chunks of night run aground in the day, that man thinks she is silent because she is giving in to her sorrow; he thinks she has decided to let death slowly fill her. That man talks to her as if he's been promised eternity.

"You know, Virginie, I see you every day, several times a day, and I tell you, after I've hunted and watched animals die, I look at you when I come back to the cabin, and in your eyes I see something like the sadness I've noticed in the animals I've killed. When I see that sadness in your eyes I ask myself if you're a little animal that's letting itself slip into death. If I knew you were dropping into a very deep well that you couldn't get out of, I wouldn't let you go down alone, Virginie, I'd go with you, and I'd try to tie myself tight to something so I could help you get out again. Virginie, all this silence puts a lot of sadness on your face, and that sadness makes you look like a tired old woman at the end of her life. You've fallen into a well of sadness, Virginie, and I'm going down there with you. Me though, I'm not sad, I'm fastened on tight at the top, and now I'm telling you, you mustn't go down too deep. I want you to come back up to the surface with me, Virginie, into life. We've had a great misfortune, but you mustn't keep dropping deeper and deeper into unhappiness every day. You must get a good grip on life. Me, I'm attached to our cabin. One day, Virginie, when the ice is gone from our inside walls, we'll build a house. I'm attached to those spruce trees as tall as ten men that I'm going to fell; I'm attached to the stumps that you and I, Virginie, we're going to pull out with the ox that I'll buy after I've sold some wood; I'm attached to the land that we'll wrench from the forest. Virginie, I'm climbing down into your well of silence and I'm offering you my hand to help you out. Cling to me, because I've got a good grip on life. We've has a great misfortune, Virginie, we can't erase that: it left a mark on our souls like a brand on an animal. It's just that, with animals, the pain only lasts as long as the hot iron's writing on their flesh, while for us, Virginie, for you and me the pain will last forever, as if we'd swallowed a chunk of iron that'll be red hot for eternity. I understand you, you see, but you mustn't kill yourself with sadness, Virginie. You mustn't drown yourself in silence. You must cry out, here in the vast white winter, that we're alive. We must cry out to the trees that we've come here to fell them. We must cry out to the frozen earth that we've come here to sow it. We must cry out to the animals that we've come here to hunt them and feed ourselves on the flesh of their young. We've known great misfortune, Virginie, but our life can go on."

She does not listen to him. She does not look at him. She does not see him. She does not hear him. But he is talking. Never has he talked so much. He has never known such a desire to talk. He has always been a man of deeds, not words. Is it because the nights are too vast around a man and a woman who are alone?

* * * * *

There is no window in the cabin. A square has been cut into the log wall; it has been closed up for the winter with moss-chinked boards, then covered with cloth. It is always night in the cabin. The stove sends soft flashes of fire onto the walls, but if Virginie wants to see, she lights a tallow candle. The flame sparkles, greedy and gluttonous. When Virginie extinguishes it, night returns. Have they brought enough candles? Did they lose any during the journey? Have they mislaid the mould? Whenever they run out of anything they think they lost it during the journey, somewhere in the snow. To lighten the load on the sleigh, that man jettisoned some of their baggage. They had anticipated everything that would be useful. Yet much was missing. He'd had to throw many sacks into the forest. Would they have tallow candles for the whole winter? The game is so lean at this time of year. March is nearly over and from time to time the April sun is triumphant in the sky. Virginie opens the door and sees trees still snugly wrapped in snow. She watches the sun kindle a square of light on the ground; in it she warms her feet, still paralyzed with cold. The hard-packed floor is like ice. Neither the leather slippers over her woollen socks, nor the dried moss stuffed into her boots, protect her feet. Virginie rarely leaves the cabin. Her feet are suffering as if she had walked barefoot in the snow all day. The Lady who had chains at her ankles must have been cold too. The stove is filled with wood, the flame is brisk enough to crack steel; Virginie uncovers her feet to be sure they're not bleeding. She feels something biting her ankles, as if they were in chains. She opens the door. The first rays of spring sun are beating down. She warms herself in the square of light on the hard-packed earth. The light is so bright, she shuts her eyes. Suddenly she remembers that man's voice forbidding her to leave the door open when there is a fire in the stove.

"If you do, I have to go farther and farther into the snow, Virginie, under the big trees, to find the dead wood that will be willing to give us fire. If the wood won't give us fire, we'll freeze to death, Virginie, both of us, here in the midst of all this snow and all these trees. We'll have to burn our cabin, one log at a time, to warm ourselves. Summer doesn't seem to be in any hurry. Up here, wood's more precious than gold. The fire in our stove is like the sun in our cabin; but it's a fragile sun. We mustn't waste the fire; so don't leave the cabin door open, Virginie, not when there's wood burning in the stove."

The wood and the fire will last until it is time for that man to die. Following her urge, Virginie pulls the door shut. Night has returned to the cabin; it is dark, as dark as it must have been in the dungeon cell of that Lady in the old, old story she's thought about so often these past days. She trembles now as she used to tremble in the past whenever she heard the story.

*   *   *   *   *

20

On the bridge of the ship the Lady was no longer cold. She huddled against the folds of the cloak that had been thrown over her shoulders. It was trimmed with elegant passementerie. The Lady must have felt the warmth toward which Virginie extends her bare feet. The new sun is melting the frost that had formed between flesh and bones during the journey in the cart, under a sky heavy with clouds that drowned the sun, under winds that descended from the small valleys between the cliffs, then disappeared in the sea. On moonless nights when sky and earth seemed to have disappeared, the soldiers would take possession of the bodies of the chained girls, sniggering, blaspheming, grunting like pigs. The girls would weep, without cries or sighs or tears, their cold dry sorrow enclosing their hearts in a numb pain that wouldn't let them love or hate. The Lady in the rich person's cloak must have shivered when the boat was loading and a soldier, whose face and clothing made him resemble those soldiers who surrounded the cart filled with girls in chains, held out his arms to her: her heart must have leaped, the blood must have shuddered as it coursed through her veins; she could not back off. She must have let herself drop into the ship whose masts were swaying in the sky. This meant freedom, a new life. Here on the gangway, the Lady was like a child about to be born. The dungeon cell was a mother in pain who now would give birth to a free child. Uttering her first cry in this new life, she was thrown into the arms of the soldier, whose odor reminded her of a barrel of salt fish at the market. Big hands clutched but did not crush her, then gently set her down on the bridge of the ship. The soldier hadn't said a single vulgar word, nor had he laughed like a hungry roaring beast. She stood on the ship that would take her to the other shore. Her life would be erased by these waves. Over there, she would begin anew. Under the boat, she felt the breathing of the sea. Her feet were set free. The ship pitched and tossed. So many people were bustling about with their burdens. She had been alone for so long. The sky was so immense. Bundles dangling from cables whirled round. The unknown country where she was being taken, so far away, made her dizzy. She was standing now, but she didn't dare to walk, as if it were still forbidden. She felt intoxicated. She knew what intoxication was. So long ago, she had been forced to drink. The more she drank, the drunker were the men around her. Could all the waves in the sea ever erase that inn where, without chains, she had been more a prisoner than in her dungeon cell? The Lady would never forget the inn, or her solitary cell. Never. Even if the new country was so far away that the past could be dissolved in it, even if the long sea-crossing would purify her memory, she would not forget her cell, or the inn where all the men were like the soldiers around the cart; nor would she forget that when she was drunk she had felt the floor of the inn trembling under her feet as the master slurped the soup in which she had poured the poison. She knew how to kill a man.

She was so young, she was only a child. Can someone still be a child if she knows how to kill a man? The master of the inn was dead. She had killed him. She had wanted to kill him. She had bought and paid for the secret that kills a man. She had watched the master of the inn writhe in pain; she had seen his desperate fingers try to rip open his belly and tear out his entrails that the poison had set ablaze. She had watched his final agony without dizziness or regret. The sea would not erase this memory. The new country could not abolish the strange night when she had experienced undying pleasure. Her feet were bare on the floor polished by salt water and she dared not step forward. For so many years, she had walked only when someone pushed her or whipped her. Here, wearing a rich woman's cloak, on the ship that was taking her to a new life, she was waiting for some harsh treatment. The soldier studied her. She seemed exhausted. The soldier was surprised that a great lady could be so tired. Her face was creased like that of someone who hasn't slept for a long time. Though she was wearing a rich cloak, the lady had no shoes. The soldier could not explain this. Here was a grand lady in bare feet, who had arrived at the ship with the girls in chains. Either she was one of them and had stolen the cloak, or she was a rich lady who had committed a crime so great that she couldn't be saved from prison. The soldier studied her again. Her feet weren't delicate feet accustomed to dainty shoes. Then she was not a great lady from whom a soldier takes his eyes only when ordered by his captain. Her hair wasn't powdered or adorned with jewels. It was the hair of a poor girl who has been wandering in rain that never ends. The cloak wasn't creased. The Lady did not move. The soldier tried to probe the mystery of this Lady with bare feet. Suddenly he spoke to her. He spoke without insulting her, he spoke without contempt, he issued no commands. He spoke to her like a woman, not a beast who mustn't disobey.

"I'm going to the New World. They're giving me land in the New World. People who're starving to death here will live like kings in the New World. Mademoiselle, I don't want to spend my whole life marching. Will I still be able to march when I'm old and lame? I'm going off to the New World to live like a king. If you, with all respect, if you aren't a wealthy lady, and if the ship gets across the sea without being torn apart by storms, Mademoiselle, I offer to be your man and protect you. I invite you to come and live with me on the land they're going to give me in the New World; I'm sure I'd like to fill my land with the children that I'd make with you, Mademoiselle, if you're not a high-born, wealthy lady. That's why, if this ship gets to the New World and you and I are still alive on the other side of the sea, I want you to know, Mademoiselle, that I intend to ask for your hand like a good Catholic, when we arrive in the New World."

*　*　*　*　*

"I think you're inventing a story and I'd like to know what it is. Just what are you thinking about, Virginie, in the cabin far from the sun? The fire's out, the door's shut, what do you think about, all hunched over with your chin on your knees, like a baby still waiting to be born. You're so sad, Virginie, as if it was autumn, though it will soon be spring. I found a river out back there; as soon as the ice is melted I'll bring you trout the size of rabbits, Virginie, and a few months after that we'll have vegetables, carrots, potatoes, that we've sown in our own land. That's what you ought to be thinking about. Look at the road that's before us, Virginie, not the one that lies behind. It's cold in the cabin. You must've been dreaming for a long time, because the fire's been out for a long time; the stove is cold. You must dream a lot, Virginie, if you forget to stir up the fire. I'll light it. And I'll open the door to let in some light. Forget the road behind us. We had some bad luck, but there may be some happiness waiting on the road that lies ahead. And what we've lost, perhaps we could, if you wanted . . . . Virginie, the past is what no longer exists. Living in the past is no life: it's death, or wanting to die . . . . You and I, Virginie, were born to live. The two of us here, in our cabin, are going to look out the open door and watch spring arrive. That's our future: felled trees, uprooted stumps, tilled soil; and every year, more trees to fell, more stumps to uproot, more soil to till. I see children, boys and girls, I see them running as I work and you're working alongside me, and animals bleating and lowing, and you and me, Virginie, tired and sweaty but happy—because we've forgotten the past. You and me, we've escaped from unhappiness. We have to forget snow and blizzards and let ourselves be touched by the spring. Soon it will be summer, Virginie, summer!"

She looks up, not at that man who talks and talks as if he were sure of living for a century, who talks of the future as if he wasn't going to die, who talks of the approaching summer as if that season weren't going to be his grave; rather, she looks at the light sparkling on the dark spruce branches and on the white snow. She cannot step out into this light, with her head high and unashamed, until she has accomplished what she must. She cannot walk in the summer light with her head high until that man is below the ground, in the grip of death where spring does not exist. He has tossed on the table a brace of hare he has trapped: every day, he brings home game. They have meat enough for a winter that would last until July. Now that spring is near, that man seems taller, his shoulders broader, and he seems full of vigor for tackling trees. By pitting himself against giant spruce trees he seems to acquire some of their strength. In the doorway, he appears a little taller each time; and each time he must bend over somewhat to enter; each time, his head is closer to the roof. As long as they've been in this forest, between winter and spring, that man has been growing as if everything he dreams of gives him strength. He has forgotten their great misfortune, now he thinks only of summer. The land to be conquered, the trees to be felled, the stones to dig out, the harvests: his dreams, a magic sap, transform him into a great tree whose tranquil branches hold no doubts. That man resembles a tree that's too strong, and Virginie will fell him. Tormented by the catastrophe, she grows thinner every day, huddled within her sorrow, but she will start to grow tall again when that man is lying on the ground, never to rise again. She is only a little woman, waiting. The trees must make way for that man who is so strong. And yet, she once saw him so destroyed, one stormy night, crushed and nearly dwarfed. That man has forgotten the catastrophe: he hunts, he kills animals and skins them so they look like naked children. He no longer thinks about that long night filled with snow as black as death; in his dreams he sees only springtime and summer. When he comes back to the cabin, bowed down by the weight of the game he amasses as if he were responsible for a large family, whose shouts fill the forest and cover the wind's tragic lament, that man despises Virginie's sorrow. He cannot understand that she can't forget; he doesn't see that her wound is still raw. He re-kindles the fire; he cares about nothing but the warmth in the cabin and the fire for cooking the meat. He stokes the fire by throwing on handfuls of bark; he pokes it. Virginie is silent. She lives in a dark prison cell, as though she had already killed. She could walk in the forest, strike up an acquaintance with the trees, discover her new country, make her way through the winter while dreaming so fervently of spring that little by little, every day would resemble it. She could dream about life, about the seeded earth, the harvests, the sun that would triumph over death; but she doesn't want to dream about life when somewhere, among trees she doesn't see, in a place that she could never find again, there occurred a death she can never forget or pardon, a death that occurred one pitch-black night when earth and heaven had both disappeared. That death demands another. Virginie will lend her hands, feverish now with the heat of July, to that death. She will kill that man who is carefully re-kindling the fire in the chilly cabin. She shudders. No one will toss a cosy woollen cloak over her shoulders. It is that man's careful work at the stove, where slowly the flame is being re-kindled, that will make her warm. That man whom she must kill will provide warmth for her cold-numbed body. She muses on the Lady who had chains at her ankles. She has thought of her story so often these past weeks! The Lady's soul is wandering among the black spruce trees. Could it have come to take refuge here in this cabin where the absence of sun and the cold, hard-packed earth recall her old prison cell? Virginie sometimes thinks she hears her breathing. She isn't worried or surprised or frightened at having decided to put her man to death. She does not pray now. She only waits. She is waiting until it is time to kill that man who has succeeded in re-kindling the fire and is smiling now with pride. Virginie is as warm as if a cloak had been thrown over her shoulders. The man rubs his hands to erase the marks left by ash and coal; now he is stroking the fur of the hare he has placed on the table: they are fat. He knows that Virginie and he will conquer winter. His body cannot contain his pride. His pride is too great for the cabin; he laughs, triumphant. She does not look at him, she is silent. That man's life has been blossoming constantly ever since he was sentenced to death. The fire has taken hold in the logs. The cast iron cracks in the heat. That man must return to the forest before daybreak. He goes out. He thinks he is leaving Virginie alone in her silence. Even though he came to re-kindle the fire, his presence has passed like a cloud. His axe begins again to crash against wood not yet thawed by the sun. The thuds that bite into the tree resound in the trunk, under the hardened bark. A muffled trembling echoes in the branches all around. In the vast silence he listens to the brief sighs, almost human, of the stricken trees. The man's repeated blows lash out at the forest. The cabin advances like a ship on the turbulent sea of black trees. The man is relentless. Virginie knows that the sound of a felling axe against wood is also the sound of the heart of this man who strikes out so as to forget death. The blows that shake the forest are her husband's voice, as the silence is the voice of her own thoughts. The fire struggles in the stove. A raging beast seems imprisoned there. The ice on the wall becomes water and trickles down. Moss in the cracks between knotty logs drips water and melting ice. All the water is running onto the dirt floor. Tonight it will be mud, or ice, for the sun will go out and winter will once more take possession of the forest. Water drips from the roof. The bed of spruce boughs will be wet tonight, like the Lady's straw mattress in her solitary cell. It rains on Virginie. The roof leaks everywhere. This water is still ice. Virginie runs outside, without closing the door. Springtime blinds her. The light is too bright. The sun is too hot. Soon it will be summer. Soon justice will be done. The felling axe shakes the tall trees. The sun has been a shock, not a caress. Virginie goes to the side of the cabin where the shadows prevail. The Lady with chains at her ankles could not leave her prison cell. Virginie still has no chains: she has pushed the door and gone out into the light. The first day of spring has tossed a cloak of harsh light over her shoulders. One day the water will drop onto Virginie, the ground will be muddy under her feet, the cold will be as avid as fire under her scorched skin and she will feel no desire to push the door: she will be, like the Lady, a prisoner. If the Lady had been able to go outside on a day like this, filled with such light, she would have gone to the shady side to look at the earth. The sun's rays turn trees and snow to fire. Virginie takes small steps in the snow, but she makes no progress. The snow drifts slowly underneath her feet. The Lady with wounded ankles would not have refused this light. But a shadow is following Virginie's steps across the snow. Is it the Lady's?

*   *   *   *   *

29

V irginie, too, has seen a soldier's arms open before her. Then the arms closed and held her against a body that throbbed with the beating of an enormous heart. Her face didn't brush against the soldier's, yet her cheeks were flushed and warm. He had said a few words, smiling. She didn't hear. Violins covered his words, but let through the cries of excited dancers. The soldier didn't smell of tobacco. Dancing was forbidden. The priests did not allow the bodies of boys ablaze with life to come too close to the bodies of girls that were ready like kindling and hoping only for fire. Alcohol too was forbidden. The men would glide hypocritically toward the door, as if that was part of the rigadoon; leaving their partners in the middle of the dance and whirling with the music, they would drift to the door and, awkwardly, go outside. When they returned, their faces lit up, eyes drowned in dream, they would rejoin the dance, but they didn't hear the music in the same way now. They had drunk alcohol. Made boisterous by Jamaica rum, they no longer danced the same dances; they were in another land, the land of alcohol, with other music, other violins; they seemed to have deserted the Mardi Gras dance; their souls were ablaze in alcohol which, if the priests were to be believed, was the Devil's fire. With his arm, the soldier held Virginie tight against his body and they whirled as fast as the music. The violins shrieked, moaned or sighed; they awakened forgotten sorrows and savage laughter. The music pierced the walls, soaring from roof to roof through the city of Quebec, it danced a jig on the roof of the church, whirled around a steeple, then skated across on the frozen St. Lawrence, finally getting lost beyond the Ile d'Orléans, in the villages scattered on the opposite shore, even into the black forests and, above them, in the distance, the horizon. The violin marked off magical notes that turned life into a dance. For Virginie and the soldier who held her in his arms, life now was nothing but a dance: the seasons, winters, tasks that strained your arms and wore out your hands, grief and sorrows, childhood distant as a dream, the future, the unknown road that would take them to old age. Life now held no concerns. The magic of the violins changed it into a heady dance. On the polished floor their matching steps marked the rhythm of their hearts. Celebrating bodies spun, unflagging. For Virginie there was no yesterday, there was no tomorrow, there was only the heart that beat in the body of the soldier who held her in his arms. Was he clinging to her so the violins wouldn't carry him off to forbidden countries? The enchanted music raised them up. They soared in those enchanted canoes of legend that followed turbulent rivers into the sky. Did the soldier's arms hold Virginie just to keep another dancer from embracing her? He had never seen this girl before on any street in Quebec and he didn't want her to dance with anyone else. Nor did he want to dance with any other girl. She was silent, as if the music could express her thoughts. Was it the furious rhythm of the dance, or the girl's body that he held too close to his own, that made his heart beat so fast? The soldier's face was

31

smiling under drops of sweat that fell onto his uniform. He seemed to be looking far off into the distance. Had he guessed that Virginie didn't want to dance in other arms? His vigor matched the fervor of the violins; he could dance as long as the violin didn't tire and fall asleep. Virginie would dance as long as the soldier held her in his arms. Unlike other boys, he sought happiness only in the music and the dance. It was enough for him to hold Virginie in his arms, while other boys would flee the dance, going out into the night, behind frosted windows where they were summoned by the fire of Jamaica rum. They would come back to the dance, their laughter like hiccups. Staggering, the boys would return, sated with rum, amazed to see the walls dancing a rigadoon with the ceiling.

Virginie understood why the priests prohibited dancing. She had decided she'd never obey them again. When music played, life itself was unveiled. Dancing turned winter to spring. Suddenly the sounds were no longer music, but cries, yet still they danced. Cries that must be attributed not to animals but to men. Then, frightened voices, shriller and less powerful: women's voices. The soldier took his arms from Virginie's waist; she was still possessed by the violins. Her body, drawn by the soldier's, did not want to be separated from him; he pushed her away. She saw him disappear among the bellowing boys who fell on one another, kicking. A chair crashed onto one, the other broke a broom upon a head; there was kicking and pounding. Glasses were broken against faces. There was choking and shoving, heads were smashed against floor or ceiling; throats were clutched, noses wrenched, jaws ripped open; fists slashed, feet swung out, ears and stomachs were pounded. Torsos were uncovered when shirts were torn to shreds. Were the shouts laughter or moaning? Each one struck out as if everyone was attacking him; arms swung, feet rose, bodies twisted. Virginie could no longer see her soldier. Now there was no one left standing. Legs and heads were tangled among the bodies. The women came back with buckets of snow and poured it over the trounced combatants, chuckling their amusement. The snow was tinged with blood. The men, stunned, grinned idiotically, wiping the blood from their faces, getting to their feet one by one, feeling their jaws or their legs. They limped, moaned, and rubbed their eyes, drunk and amazed. Suddenly spying a familiar face, a friend, a buddy, they bellowed their surprise as if they hadn't seen each other for a long time, and fell into each other's arms, hugging, embracing. Bleeding, wounded, their limbs sore, their shirts torn over scratched flesh, they went outside, entwined, to drink Jamaica rum. Wasn't it Mardi Gras? The soldier didn't go out with the others. He came back to Virginie. He wasn't bleeding. He wasn't hurt. His frock-coat was spotless. He held out his arms as if nothing had happened and closed them around Virginie. He led her to the middle of the room. Virginie saw some women whispering about her; it mattered so little. Softly the violins began to sing again. It seemed to Virginie that the soldier and she had never stopped dancing. She could feel the soldier's heart beat in her own body. The violins' melody quickened again. All of life was dancing along with them. Suddenly the soldier spoke.

"I haven't asked your name yet, Mademoiselle, and I know it's very impolite to dance with a young lady and not be able to say her name, but you must believe me, I'm reeling so, I forgot to ask what you wanted me to call you."

"Virginie."

"Well now, Mademoiselle Virginie, I won't be wanting to dance with anyone but you."

"And you Monsieur, what's your name?"

"My troopers call me Sergeant, my superiors call me Sergeant, the innkeeper calls me General. I've almost forgotten that my mother and father gave me the name of Victor. So, Virginie, you can call me Victor."

"Why did you fight?"

"If I was a liar, Virginie, I'd tell you it was because one of those boors had dared to look at you . . . ."

Virginie felt her face scalding under the rice powder she had applied with so much care. The soldier, too, had turned red.

"But I'm not a liar, Mademoiselle Virginie, so I'll just tell you that fighting to a soldier is like embroidery to a woman. And I'll even tell you that for a soldier, fighting is as natural as sleeping and eating. In fact, I'd say that a soldier who doesn't fight, Mademoiselle Virginie, is only good for hanging on the wall inside a frame. Fighting's almost as good as dancing . . . . "

"Since you'd just as soon grab other savages by the throat as dance with me, I'm not dancing any more."

She reared up inside the iron ring that the soldier's arms formed around her waist. She wasn't strong enough to free herself. The tattered, merry revellers, with their young ladies, were following the rhythm of music they alone could hear. Was it not Mardi Gras? And after this day would come Lent, seven long weeks filled with the sorrow of Christ dying on his cross. She eyed the soldier with contempt.

"Let me explain, Mademoiselle Virginie."

She stood there stiffly (like a soldier).

"I told you, Mademoiselle Virginie, that for a soldier fighting's natural. A soldier's a man who wants to fight another man. A soldier who'd rather dance than fight is an ambassador, not a sergeant. That's the truth, Mademoiselle Virginie. If you don't punish me by being grumpy just because I told you the truth . . ."

He stood at attention as if he were facing a general, but his arms were around Virginie. She launched another salvo, which he wasn't expecting.

"If you talked less to horses and more to girls, you'd know that modern girls prefer little lies to big truths. Excuse me, but I must go home now, before the devil comes looking for me, with his beaver hat and his fiery carriage. Fight well."

"Mademoiselle Virginie..."

He couldn't hold her back. He realized that she, too, enjoyed a fight. He opened his arms. She took her fur coat. Over the dancers' heads and over the wild music of the violins, the soldier exclaimed:

"Tomorrow, Virginie, on the Place du Marché, our platoon is performing an exercise. If you want to see me, come! Place du Marché!"

She had already gone out, wrapped snugly in her coonskin coat. Her faithful, protective chaperone followed. Virginie glanced in the window. Not all the panes were frosted over. Among the dancers whirling in a disorder that the music seemed to enjoy, she spotted the soldier, the Sergeant, Victor, his body stiff as a sword, arms outstretched as if she was coming back to hurl herself inside them.

* * * * *

L ike a lightning bolt in the trunk. It seems that the tree, motionless despite its wound, will not fall. Virginie knows those silences now, quieter than the usual silence of forest and snow. Then a muscle shatters in the spruce. Another muscle breaks inside the wood. The tree will bend. Finally, a single break and all its muscles burst. The tree falls: air whistles through the branches. A brief sigh. Other, more pitiless cracks ring out. Branches collide, entwine and grip the branches of nearby trees. The sap is frozen, the wood sounds like ice. The tree falls onto the snow, making a muffled sound like a sack of flour. Then its branches twist and shatter on the ground. A brief silence. The man, who had stepped back to protect himself, returns to his victim. Up to his waist in the snow, he stamps out a path all around the tree. Virginie knows that now he is tackling the branches of the spruce; he fights this forest as if it were his mission to cut down all the trees in Canada. Virginie knows there aren't many trees left to fell. It would be more sensible if he cleared only enough space to lay out his body. How can she think such things in this light that is repainting life on earth? That man's fate has been decided. She should stop thinking about punishment, and live one day at a time, like those who are not determined to bring about death. When the time comes, everything will follow in order, like summer that comes after spring and winter: in its own good time; thinking about it too much won't speed up the time of justice; on the contrary, thinking about it too much will stretch out the weeks and the months, for every thought is a beat of time that takes its own place in time. The Lady who had chains at her ankles must have dreamed a great deal too. When the time has come, this man's stricken body will be exposed to the teeth of wild animals that will tear the flesh from his bones. Let them carry his bones to their burrows! Let his bones be scattered through the forest and gnawed. And let no one know that they are the scraps of a man! She will render justice. Neither other men nor other women have the right to render justice. Virginie will be condemned to prison like the Lady. Instead of stretching out at the moment when this man is confronting the truth of his own death, time is now reaching back toward a past as distant as a dying echo. Today, here in this sunlight, the shadow that accompanies her across the snow, around the birchbark-covered cabin, is not her own body's shadow, but the Lady's. If she could listen, if only the silence of snow and trees prevailed, if the axe weren't striking out relentlessly, furiously, at the trees, she would hear the sound of the shadow's chains across the snow. She thinks of a lady held captive, but through the fabric of her clothing the light is as mild as a memory of summer. She dreams of a prison cell, but the space around her is as vast as the infinite sky; she could walk for weeks and months and still not reach its limits. She could end up in the land of the dead and never come to the limit of this forest. Virginie doesn't want to advance any further in this ocean of trees. She walks around the cabin. The silence is weighed down by all the mute branches and all the tree trunks that cling to the earth under the snow, with their mute and persistent desire to live. The indifferent forest prevails as if Virginie didn't exist. To justify his existence, that man grapples with space; he counts the trees he has felled, he fights a battle that sends off echoes of quivering blows: he exists! He strikes out at space, he shakes it, while Virginie, her eyes dazzled, is frail, small and useless. But when that man falls, something important will happen among the tangled trunks and branches. She must kill him so that she will exist. Through an ineluctable law to which her blood is submissive, to which her soul is submissive as one day she herself was submissive to life and as she will be submissive to death, Virginie will kill that man, to wound the forest. She will let the forest know that she exists, for she will have given the forest the strongest blow that she can deal: a man's death. Simply by thinking about it, she exists. And where there is nothing but the frozen silence of black treetrunks and branches, there too she feels she exists. In this forest that reduces everything to silence, Virginie will kill. She will hide this secret inside the inviolable secret of the slow growth of trees. Through the blow she will inflict on that man, Virginie will declare that she is a woman amid these indifferent trees, a woman who suffers, a woman who wants to live; that is why she will kill. Ineluctably, summer will punish winter. The cabin is adrift, minuscule, vulnerable, amid the ages heaped up on the ground. Thinking of the death she will deal out, Virginie feels alive, as she was on the day she gave birth: she felt then that the world existed only so she could give birth. When she thinks of the death she will deal out, everything is explained. Virginie exists, as truly as a beating heart. She is surrounded by strange trees, black and motionless; she is surrounded by unfathomable snow, surrounded by silence, so that she can deal out death. Here in the silence the Lady who is dragging her chains, joins past and future together. Through the act of death, the Lady who is Virginie's shadow, who is present as a lingering thought, will suddenly take shape in the present age. And Virginie, who is walking now in the sun, will then become a memory. A painful flash goes through her head: is it April that has dazzled her?

* * * * *

Streaming with sweat from the dance, Virginie hastens to follow her zealous chaperone who is muttering how late it is for a young lady with a good Catholic upbringing: too late on the eve of the Lenten penitence, when a true Christian must prepare himself through pitiless fasting to die with Christ for his sins and to be resurrected with Him on Easter morning. Virginie, her chaperone reproached her, had danced with gusto the priests would not have allowed, if ever they had dared to permit dancing. Virginie laughed at her chaperone's discomfiture. She had danced, it was true, the way a drunkard long deprived of alcohol might have drunk. She looked again, through frost-covered window-panes, at the soldier who was surprised to be no longer dancing. Her chaperone's reproaches sounded funny. She had the easy laughter that comes with wine, but she hadn't drunk; she had only danced and her body was drunk. She had danced so much that it was hard to walk; her legs seemed to want to obey only the dance of the violins, refusing to submit to the rhythm of the footsteps heading for her father's house. Her muscles were commanding her to dance, but she must go home. Like the Lady who was boarding the ship, a soldier had held out his arms to her. No doubt all these soldiers looked alike: chests puffed out, muscles tense, straight as swords and, inside flesh they thought was like steel, the tenderness of a child seeking the warmth of the breast. Virginie had danced on a night inhabited by demons struggling to make Mardi Gras last into Lent. She remembers that she didn't fear the arrival of the Inspector from Hell who comes in his fiery chariot to visit balls that go on too long. Virginie looks at her shadow on the snow: there seem to be chains clanking at her feet.

*   *   *   *   *

Virginie did not go to the Place du Marché to admire the military review—all gleaming rifles and horses brushed so carefully that they, too, seemed to be in uniform. She stayed at home, sitting at the window. The light that fell on her embroidery brought with it some of the greyness of the walls. She wasn't bored. Life seemed to have stopped with the beginning of Lent. The street was deserted. The inhabitants of the city had shut themselves inside their houses to pray. A touch of regret pricked at her forehead, but she applied herself to her embroidery: this fairy stitch required a good deal of concentration and the thread was very fine. She had started this work some time ago, devoting her quiet Sunday afternoons and winter evenings to it, while she waited for sleep. She was copying the gestures and the patience of her mother who, when she was Virginie's age, had also started to embroider a tablecloth. A young woman must bring her husband an embroidered tablecloth to be spread upon the table for grand occasions, several times in her life.

And after the death of the embroiderer, who had since become an old woman and a grandmother, perhaps even a great-grandmother, the cloth would be found, folded in a drawer and scented with violets, and the women would exclaim, enraptured, at the work that had gone into it. They would express regret: "Young people don't have patience like that nowadays; young people have lost all the talents of our race!" and they would be astonished at the skill of the embroiderer who employed stitches that were no longer known. "Grandmother did that before she was married!" someone would exclaim. In the tablecloth, written in knots and flowers of thread, there would be a testament where the deceased set down her expectations of the female descendants who would inherit it. The cloth, suddenly heavy, would be piously put away in its drawer. The woman who was going to inherit it would agree to continue the life of the one who was gone. Virginie embroidered. She was thinking, a little, of all those things. Her mother, who like her was bent over a piece of fine handiwork, must be thinking the same thoughts as Virginie. Her mother, too, had once been a girl. In a few years Virginie would become a woman: a woman with a rounded belly and a swollen face, where youth would fade into a small submissive pain. Mystery of ever-changing life: a girl will be an old woman and an old woman was once a girl. Only the religiously embroidered tablecloth would not change: wrapped in blue paper, it would scarcely turn yellow. The light was rather sad. Her silent mother's thoughts had taken her to another time, and the house was so quiet it seemed not to exist: there was no creaking of rusty nails, no moaning of dowels or beams; the house seemed dead. Virginie, somewhat dazed by the light as she had been intoxicated by the music of the violins, somewhat dazed too by the movement of needle and thread, as if they were possessed by the dance, had her head filled with a feast of thoughts that danced in the mist.

The magic of knots and loops created pretty flowers on the linen. The nuns in the convent had taught her that life, like thread, is nothing by itself, but in the hands of a skillful, industrious, tenacious girl, it can become an inspired flower. She heard again melodies from the dance the night before, soaring above the night, echoing in the day, whirling in her head. Sitting on her straw-bottomed chair, from time to time she felt the soldier's arms around her. She was sorry she hadn't gone to the Place du Marché, to the military demonstration, but she was happy, too, that she hadn't accepted the militiaman's invitation. Let him strut about, with his chest puffed out, his chin jutting toward the horizon: she wasn't there. He was probably looking for her as he clutched his rifle, walked stiff-legged, held his head high and clicked his heels, but he wouldn't find her. She was proud she hadn't obeyed that man. She smiled at the thought as she bent over her embroidery on which a ray of light—grey dust, a minuscule dry rain—was falling. That was how the sun always appeared in this small street hollowed out at the bottom of the cliff. And yet, on the Place du Marché, the snow was white and the sun was blazing. Forty days before Easter the sun baked the soldiers' faces and blinded them while they must remain standing for a long time, motionless as stones. Their rifles flashed in the sun. Virginie's father, who had watched the demonstration, came home with his face reddened by the sunlight reflected off the white mirror of the snow. He told some stories, the same ones he always told. When he was young he had carried a rifle and "If you didn't have a rifle, you used sticks. We weren't the sort of militiamen who look like a row of fancy candies in a beribboned box. We were soldiers who fought like Indians, using tactics from the woods. Today's soldiers have never seen an Indian and I wonder if they'd know a spruce tree from a lamp post. But they're clean, our militiamen. Much too clean to fight! They're as clean as the Anglais. They have cute little rifles they only fire on

Sunday — and then they're blanks so they won't scare anybody! But they have glory: their bodies are as stiff as fence pickets and they look out into the distance, far above humanity. When they march, hundreds of militiamen march as if the platoon had just two arms and two legs, that's how well they obey their leader. In our day, everybody had his own two hands and his own two feet. When you fired your rifle, you fired into the crowd, every one of you; you'd hit as many as you could, you didn't wait for a Royal command either. When it came time to clear out, we didn't have the patience to wait for the next fellow to turn left so we could follow him, on the same foot. Today, with the music and all the militiamen marching in step, with the drums and uniforms and cannon shots and rifle volleys and the sun shining on the uniforms and weapons, it was a fine sight; but if you ask me, a soldier's an even finer sight when he's covered with mud from the ground he's taken from the Anglais." Virginie went on with her embroidery. She congratulated herself for not having gone to the Place du Marché to see her dancing partner. Later, though, she joined a group of girls in their Sunday-best cloaks, who were going to a religious service. They asked if she'd gone to the military ceremony. In their eyes there was some of the wonder they'd brought back from the Place du Marché and, about their lips, a certain happiness because they'd seen so many strong and handsome lads who could fight and kill if they had to. The girls reproached her for her absence, with sorrowful conviction. During the prayers and singing that reeked of incense, Virginie was sorry she hadn't gone to see her dancer, her soldier.

*   *   *   *   *

Virginie will kill that man. Her life will not be like her mother's. The virtues learned from embroidery, she'll apply to the death of that man. When he awakened, when he went to open the door to see what the weather was like, hoping to open it on the light of another spring day, winter sprang at him, like something that will endure. He needed all his strength to push the door shut. No, it wasn't spring. The floor of the cabin had turned to ice again. Victor regretted once more that he hadn't covered the bare earth with young spruce trunks, then filled the cracks with moss. There were so many urgent tasks: wild animals to hunt for food, wood to cut for fire and trees to fell so that in the spring, when the snow had disappeared, he could uproot stumps and pull out stones and prepare the earth to receive the first sowing of buckwheat, oats and alfalfa. Winter has once more tightened its grip on the land. The North wind is unleashed in a cavalcade: the boles of the great black spruce bow under the passage of the frenzied snow. Victor recounts how, in the West, where there are vast unwooded spaces, great dizzying plains, people fought on horseback and one might see the approach of a big cloud running along the earth; and it was only after you had been engulfed in the cloud that you realized it was full of Indians and horses. Once the cloud had gone by, only desolation was left on the plain. That was the story today's blizzard reminded her of, this snowstorm that raged like the one on the day of their catastrophe. The snow pushes at the door, creeps between the door and the log at the threshhold. They are safe. Don't they have a roof over their heads and walls around them? Don't they have a fire? Don't they have wood? Oh, on the day of their catastrophe, if they'd had walls and a roof, if they'd had fire, they would have been protected! The door is barricaded now, propped up by a log. He has thrown logs into the stove, the fire is hungry and the great wind blows through the walls. Victor stirs up the coals. He piles on some logs: they're not as dry as they should be.

They must be arranged with knowing precision so the air can help the fire grip the wood. Oh, on the day of their catastrophe, if they'd had dry logs, fire, a wall, they would have been stronger . . . . That man talks and talks . . . . He always says what's going on in his head or in his heart; every one of his thoughts turns to words. He talks endlessly; when he's alone in the forest he must share his thoughts with the trees. Virginie, though, is silent. She is always silent. As if she had lost the power of speech on the day of their catastrophe. That night she screamed, she screamed, not just hard enough to tear her throat apart (blood had come to her lips from shrieking her pain), but hard enough to rend the indifferent night. She cried out her pain like a Christ with no cross, whose Father in Heaven did not want to hear. Ever since, she has been silent. In the militia, that man had known a soldier who lost the power of speech when he was hit on his head: he had utterly forgotten human language and when he did try to speak, childish gibberish would issue from the bottom of his throat. Pain had the same effect on Virginie, or so that man had thought at first. Then, little by little, he realized that Virginie did not speak to him because she had decided not to. She had decided after the catastrophe that silence is louder than the harshest reproaches. She stopped talking to him and he walked out of her life. She has already killed him with her silence. Even if the putting-to-death has not yet taken place, his death has truly occurred. She sees him, in his human form, wearing clothes that she folded and put in the canvas sack before they set out on their journey: he stirs up the fire, kneeling before the stove, but he is already dead. If he talks, he talks like the dead whose words often come to join with the words of the living. Virginie is silent. Virginie does not listen to that man who is always talking. He is dead and he talks constantly to drive back the silence. Virginie wouldn't even want to listen to that man's silence, if he were suddenly to fall silent. She knows all his words, she knows all his thoughts: always harping on the same thing. She also knows his promises: he tells of fields of oats, of carrots, carrots that taste of honey, of cows and milk; he promises her a straw mattress, hens that will cheep around the cabin, eggs to be gathered from under their warm bellies, a horse for the heavy chores, a window with panes of glass, a wood floor over the hard-packed earth, cloth for sewing a new skirt and, later, a real house, painted outside and in; that man makes promises as if he weren't about to die; he doesn't remember the past, there is only the future, for him there is no more winter, he knows only the summer that will come from the other side of spring; he is a man who does not remember, who doesn't know what tomorrow will bring. Virginie no longer listens to him, but she hears him all the same, when he goes far away to hunt or marks the boundaries of his property in the bark of trees, or when his axe rings out against the frozen trunks of trees. He talks endlessly. Virginie's silence is present everywhere, like winter; it seeps inside him, he says, and it has a bitter taste. The silence hurts him. But that man, who does not remember the past and knows only the future, thinks that her silence will pass like the icy season and that there is springtime in the air, where words will blossom once again. He doesn't accept this silence which has invaded their life. And yet, it will continue to weigh on him, more and more implacable. That man does not admit death. He thinks his own is still far away, at the end of a number of seasons that will follow one another. Forgetfulness has fallen over his catastrophe, like a trail of snow. Now he would like to make a child. Bestowing life does not erase death. He explains that the child could be born in the winter. An infant's cries ringing out in the snow-covered forest could never erase the silence of the other child. The winter is fierce. Gusts of wind pound at the cabin. The gnarled branches moan. Virginie is silent. Until the storm is over and the man can open the door again and, with his axe and rifle over his shoulder, disappear into the trees that will stand straight again once peace is restored, she will stay with him, shut up in this prison cell. He burns wood as stubbornly as someone who would heat up the entire universe. Even if the flame melted the stove, even if it warmed the wind that seeps in between the logs, even if their entire bodies sweated, in the cabin there will always be the cold of Virginie's silence. Man and woman, face to face, in the midst of a raging storm, both of them close to the fire: one who speaks endlessly, the other who is silent; man and woman alone in the middle of the forest, where the wind sweeps the snow as it did on the day of their catastrophe; man and woman in the mystery that condemns them to death, one on the imminent day she will have chosen, the other in a damp cell, on straw, that will be chosen by God; man who speaks and whose words are already the silence of one who is no longer there, woman who says nothing and whose silence becomes torture; man who hopes, woman who despairs: they are safe here, beside a well-fed fire, but they are lost, body and soul, somewhere in the storm; they struggle against the wind, they are apart, they are alone. The snow confuses earth and sky. Death is hidden in these gusts. What will it take from them? This cabin made of moss-chinked logs and covered with birchbark is the cell where Virginie awaits her end. Virginie, like the Lady, has been condemned to wear chains. She will kill a man. She remembers things that are part of the Lady's memory. As a child she wept so much because of the heavy chains that hurt the Lady's feet.

*   *   *   *   *

48

"I f you wanted, Virginie, we could have a child, but only if you wanted. It's natural to have a child. When a man and woman are together they shouldn't stay alone, children should spring up around them like beautiful flowers from the good Lord that later will become little men and little women, who will continue life and cause more little men and women to flower. That's the law of life, Virginie. The good Lord wants life to continue. You mustn't stop life. A man and woman mustn't live together as if they didn't know God's law, or as if God didn't exist. Making children is the reason the good Lord put men and women on this earth; if the good Lord hadn't wanted children He'd have covered the earth with bears and oxen and cows .... Virginie, if the good Lord had wanted only stones on the earth, He'd have created nothing but stones. There's one law in this life: it says that a man and woman should make children. Well then, you and me, we're a man and a woman, so why don't you want to make a child together? We could do it now, in the spring, the end of winter, and the child would come at the start of next winter. Virginie, we could make the child today, because I'm not going out in that storm. We could make a child right now! I've put dry wood on the fire. While the fire crackles and makes pretty sparks, you and I could be obeying God's law. I won't always be able to do all the work to enlarge our land, I'll need strong arms to help me. And this land, once she's been cleared and she's like a fine fat pregnant woman, and once my arms give out on me, well then I'd like to have a child I could hand myself over to, and you too, and our land. You need children to pass on your life to; otherwise why are we on this earth? I know that you're thinking about a child too. You're a woman, Virginie, and a woman, like a man, hasn't many things to think about besides a child. You're thinking about a child who's behind us, in the snow of time past, while I'm thinking of a child who's waiting for us somewhere in the snow of time to come. We lost a child. Do you think that all the children of the bears or all the children of the wolves or all the children of the birds live long enough to make children? Do you think that all the children who are born can live out their lives to the end? The good Lord made the law. In his law, many children have to die. That's because the good Lord wants us to make even more children. I wouldn't want us just to stand there looking at our tragedy, the way you'd look at a well that seems to be getting drier and drier. We have to continue along our way. We must make a child to take our revenge on the great winds sent by the good Lord. You must cry, Virginie, because losing a child is sad. It's like dying a little yourself; it's a bit of your own life that dies. You must cry because death is sad. No one ought to die. Especially not children, and most of all not small children who haven't yet known the happiness of running in the summer sun, under the good Lord's great skies. It's sad, but it's the good Lord's law that children die as often as old people. The good Lord who created the earth and who makes winters and summers, must know what He's doing, but me, I don't understand and neither do you, and you don't say anything and you weep in your soul, you say nothing as if the time had already come to cover your lips with the silence that freezes the mouths of the dead. Children die everywhere, Virginie. In all the houses along the road that brought us here, children have died. On the door of every house there's a little nail where a black ribbon was hung when a child died in that house. Death is God's law, Virginie, but we should be thinking about life. And it's also God's law that where death has passed, a man and woman should sow life. Virginie, there's a storm raging outside, there's a warm fire in the cabin, we could make a child; he'd be as strong as the storm, and his soul would be as warm as the fire in the stove."

* * * * *

We know our future as well as our past, but we'd rather live as if we knew neither the one nor the other; we walk on this earth with our ankles bound by the chains of the past. Virginie knows that now. The crows have returned. They're cawing above the forest. The strong April light will conquer winter as it has always done. The cabin is like a boat gradually approaching the shores of spring. In the summer she will kill a man. She has already killed him in her soul. This future fact is already a past fact. That man, who set out with his axe across muddy earth where the snow has disappeared and left meandering streams, is the memory of a man who was alive. In olden days the Lady too had killed a man. Could it be that the weight Virginie has felt in her legs ever since she decided to kill her man is the weight of the Lady's chains? Soon the man will fall down into the grass and moss. Will it be Virginie or the Lady who deals the fatal blow? Why will she kill him? The reasons are written far away, beyond her soul, beyond her life, beyond her own time.

Perhaps Virginie was alive at the time of the Lady, who is still alive during this spring that is awakening the tree under which that man will fall. Was it in July that she put an end to her man? Would Virginie remember? Virginie's memory ranges wider than her life. Would she remember the future as well? Virginie thinks too much. She feels the earth breathe under her feet. All these ideas daze her. Even though it is spring the man has not unblocked the window. Inside the cabin it is not so dark as in winter, but night still prevails. The stove throws flashes of light on the walls. Lost in thought, she is dazzled as if she had walked out into the full April sunlight. But she does not go out. She doesn't want to walk around the cabin any more; the earth is as muddy as it was in the Bible, before the dry land was divided from the waters. Victor has covered the muddy floor with branches on which she must step so as not to sink in. The wet wood is slippery. She must wear boots thickly coated with mink oil. The mud wets her long skirt and it sticks coldly to her legs. She does not open the door to the light. She opens it only when that man returns. She barricades herself against the forest filled with silence, wild animals, mysteries, the unknown. He realizes that she is afraid. So then he explains that if Virginie would only go out into the light of spring, that light would wash away her fear, just as it makes the snow disappear. "Spring," he said, "works miracles." He shows her the sugary water he has collected from his maples. He will boil it up. It will become syrup and sugar to spread on bread. Virginie is afraid. That man tells her she thinks too much. She is dumbfounded by her thoughts. Soon summer will come. The hard tasks will require her arms. She will help him to roll away the big stones, to uproot stumps; she will pick up pebbles, saw wood, scatter seed; he will hold the reins of the horse, if they can replace the one that fell in the storm. All the work to be done on the land will give her less to think about than snow that settles dizzily onto the ground, then spreads out and reflects a white light in which everything is erased. Every night she will be able to see the marks left by her toil; the next day other tasks will leave other traces and, whatever the wind, night will not erase what has been done during the day. Absorbed in her work, she will be less afraid. The snow all around her and the forest heavy with silence, the awakening past, the great catastrophe that swooped down on them, all have sown such disorder within her that she is, at the same time, as young as a child and as old as the memory of another time. She is as fearful as a hare that hears footsteps. And yet, she knows she will kill that man. She is a young woman in a cabin that sits on the earth, yet she trembles with fear, she is shaken as if she was being swept away on a raging sea. She remembers a time when her body and her thoughts were churned by disorderly swirls: the day when she gave birth to the child. Today, in this season which gives life to summer, Virginie will not give birth. Does her dizziness come from the death she will deal out? This time Virginie will bring forth death. Is it so very different? Giving life has led her to giving death. Virginie trudges along the logs scattered over the muddy earth. That man promised to bring more spruce boughs tonight, that he would spread over the ground to soak up the mud. She has too many thoughts for such a young woman. Her thoughts are too dark for a day in spring. She is incapable of not thinking them. She cannot go out into the new light and simply welcome it. She stays in the cabin. For several days now she has not gone out. She would like to wait, and go out only to bestow death. But they must play this game, as if he weren't going to die, they must sow as if he would still be alive for the harvest. For doesn't life consist of accomplishing tasks just as if we weren't doomed to die! And if she acts as if she weren't going to kill that man, wouldn't it be the best way to prepare for his death? She will kill him as if she herself weren't one day going to die. After doing what she must do, she will look up to Heaven and await its judgment: let her be struck down by God's thunder, or by a gentle summer light. In the cart that may have taken her over rugged roads to another prison cell, damper and darker perhaps, with more brutal guards, the Lady must have often questioned the torture of Heaven's silence. On the boat that brought her to the New World, she must have often raised her free woman's eyes to Heaven. A soldier had held out his arms to her and, on the bridge, he looked at her not with eyes like a fierce dog, its appetite satisfied with flesh, but with the astonished gaze of Adam in his garden, when he first saw Eve. When that man looks at her, his gaze is mild, like that of a man who has accepted death. That man's eyes are like those of a wild animal submitting to death. And yet he repeats once again that a man and a woman have been given the gift of causing life to triumph over death, joy over sorrow, the gift of replacing a dead child with a child who will be born. "A man and a woman can re-kindle a flame that's gone out, Virginie. A man and a woman are a source of life when death's somewhere around them." She is silent, she shuts her eyes. Must she believe that this springtime is real?

* * * * *

Her father talked at length about the colored uniforms on the Place du Marché and the horses that marched like well-schooled men. The orders were given in English, and the horses understood that language better than many men in the city of Quebec. Her girlfriends feverishly describe the military demonstration. The militiamen had upright, vigorous, sculpted bodies, and muscular legs that could walk to the end of the country. Their arms could break an enemy's bones, but they could also hold a girl in a dance, so gently as to make her dream. Her friends laughed as they told their story, and they sighed as well: the soldiers were handsome in their uniforms for the royal celebration. All boys, or so the girls thought, should walk with that bearing, which seemed able to pass through walls of stone. They moved forward as if no one else existed on this earth. They marched as if they hadn't seen the girls with lips as red as strawberries; they turned to the left, they turned to the right, and their eyes seemed not to see the bouquets of laughing girls. They stepped forward and back; their rhythmical movements were performed as if they were natural. Sometimes one of the damsels would swear that a militiaman had noticed her, because she'd seen a sudden redness in his face. Her companions would burst out laughing and their laughter was like the cheeping of birds on the Place du Marché, over the officer's cries. The rifles gleamed. Suddenly, the soldiers became motionless. Only the rifles seemed alive: they were pointed, thunder was about to pour from each of the little iron mouths, and people trembled as they awaited the shot. It rang out. What enemy could resist such thundering might? The detonation quivered like an echo in the girls' bodies. The soldiers, all together, set off again, as triumphant as if they'd just reduced some fortress to dust. The people gathered around felt as if something had truly been destroyed. Oh! as long as there were men like these, women would be safe. God, who created frail women, had made strong soldiers for them. Her friends described that Sunday with so many sighs, so much laughter, so many silences (as long as a dream) that Virginie was sorry she hadn't gone to the demonstration. Face down on the counterpane, she wept because she hadn't gone to the celebration. She would never see her soldier again. During the dancing he had told her his name, Victor, but she never would have dared, neither in her tears nor in her reveries, to call him that. It was customary, during Lent, to do penance for one's sins. No day should end that was not marked by some deprivation. Virginie had grown dreamy. Everything that was real for a girl, like housekeeping, marketing, mending, darning, embroidery, the laundry and the dishes, now seemed unreal; daydreaming seemed to be her one true occupation. She should have spent her day like a responsible woman; but no, she had daydreamed. Was it not a sin against the Lenten law of penitence to daydream rather than devote oneself, submissively, to the tasks the good Lord had entrusted, with love, to the girls and women in men's households? It was a sin to daydream so much. Her parents decided that, to seek forgiveness by Christ on His Cross, Virginie could not go out with these friends, who laughed too much, who trembled at the slightest breath of spring, over-eager little flowers, before the Passion. In the wind that blew across the cobblestones, onto the stones of the houses, breath chilled by the river's ice, these girls were already wearing springtime frocks, too tight at the waist, the skirts too broad and brightly colored, that were traps for boys. Their cloaks, wide open to welcome spring, showed the shape of their bodies which, according to the priests, must never be seen by man, either by day or by night. Virginie would henceforth be forbidden to join these overly happy girls who offended the laws of mortification, modesty and discretion. Now, during Lent, instead of reflecting on the pain suffered by the tortured Christ before His death on the Cross, they thought only about boys and dances and running off into the copses of the upper town, where many libertines had experienced something that ought to remain a mystery until the revelation of marriage. Virginie no longer had permission to go out with girls who laughed as if Jesus Christ weren't going to die on the Cross at the end of Lent. Her parents forbade her to have too much joy on her cheeks, at a time when fasting should fill bodies with sorrow and darken faces. These girls were dreaming of handsome boys in fine costumes like those in the American magazine that Virginie had bent over every night this week; knowing nothing, they imagined that the handsome young men in fine clothes would step off the pages of the magazines and come and kiss their hands. They were so full of imagination that they couldn't see life as it is: a road full of pitfalls and suffering and work, as the priests said, but also a road that leads to celestial paradise, for those who submissively accept the ordeals and offer up their suffering to God so that He'll forgive their sins. These girls forgot the priests' teaching and saw life before them full of fancy; such mirages warmed their senses. Virginie must be protected. During the forty days of Lent her parents forebade her to go for walks on the city streets, already alive with the sprightly hope of Spring. She was forbidden to wear her new outfits. When Christ's body was covered with sores and gaping wounds, it was no time to dress in soft velvet, with ribbons and delicate buttons and embroidery: the body must reflect the penitence imposed on it. Virginie was sad. Shut up in her parents' house, she was busy with a mother's tasks. How would she find a husband if her parents shut her in? She was truly a prisoner of her parents, condemned to forced household labor; she rubbed soiled clothes in soapy water, peeled potatoes and scrubbed the wooden floor, hurting herself on splinters, scratching herself on iron nails, burning herself with encaustic. She had been deprived of the right to devote herself to the simple joy of no longer being a child, without yet being a woman, drunk with happiness at being a girl for whom life would be finer than ever. Sitting close to her mother, generally not talking because her mother was saying the prayers she was afraid she wouldn't have time to say later, Virginie embroidered flowers on the tablecloth she would store in the big cedar chest when it was finished, while waiting for her wedding day. She would eat her first meals with her husband off this cloth, then wash it and put it away in the chest, and they wouldn't eat off it again except at the great moments in their life, such as days of birth or death. When her fingers were stiff from too much embroidering or when her eyes burned with a fire that kept her from seeing the thread on the cloth, she would take up the magazine her friends had lent her and leaf through it once more; she stopped at the fashion plates that showed what was being worn in the big cities, and lingered as she always did, contemplating these garments that were not to be seen in the city of Quebec. She wished she could understand what was written, but it wasn't her language. So she looked at the drawings. At times she would catch a word in italics, in her language. Her mother would suddenly interrupt her praying and reproach her daughter for those flighty daydreams that dazzled young girls and made them stray from the straight path the good Lord had traced. Her mother would snap at her, using words that Virginie had often heard in church, in the priest's mouth. She listened without replying. She would put down her magazine and take up her needle and hoop; her mother went back to her prayers. Virginie felt she was a prisoner, like the Lady in olden times, whose story she had heard so often, a story so old it was worn, a story torn by time, that it was impossible to understand altogether. The Lady had chains at her ankles. Perhaps Virginie wasn't really a prisoner, because she had no chains, but she must stay inside and what was there for her to do but dream? Industriously, making small stitches, she formed a flower-petal on the table-cloth. Who would eat with her from this embroidered cloth? It would take so many months to finish it, there were so many flowers and clusters to fashion from the delicate thread! But already she saw it, carefully starched, laid upon a table, with its straight folds. Before her at the table she saw the handsome soldier who had held her in his arms, the night of Mardi Gras. And yet it seemed to Virginie that the soldier existed only in her dream of that marvellous Mardi Gras dance and would never return to her real life.

*　*　*　*　*

One day that man will rush into the cabin, he will hurl himself at her and, like a thrusting dagger, plunge his seed into her belly. She will cry out, she will scratch, she will struggle; he will make her a child because that man thinks a child will have the gift of changing to flowers the crown of thorns that was placed on his wife's head one winter night. This time, he does not talk: he is wrestling, all muscles tensed, with a tree-stump, as if the stump were a living creature to be conquered. Virginie can sense, behind her, the man's obsessive desire, like a mute crouching beast, its claws poised, waiting to pounce. The man cannot see the past; for him, things cease to exist when they are erased. For him, the road opened up through the spruce trees disappeared along with the snow that had covered it, and the night when catastrophe struck has vanished with the dawn that drove it away. The man can see only the seasons that will come, the future years that will bring harvests in the bushland instead of the dense spruce trees he will fell. He wants children whose eyes will watch their father battling the forest.

He has forgotten that, in the depths of a night with no day, a child watches his father with eyes that will never see the harvests, and in the depths of the impassable night, the child can recall only an endless squall that covered him with snow that piled up on his small body, becoming as black as the darkest night. No, giving life to a child will not restore life to the one who disappeared in snows that no longer exist. She is silent. She will bestow death instead. She waits. One day he will take hold of her, to inject her with his man's seed; she will be strong, stronger than a violent man, stronger than a man inflamed by his male desire, stronger than the fierce beast inside this man. If she agrees to give life, could she ever bestow death? If she is to punish the man, she must remember the child who was lost in the blizzard. The snow is now only a cold white memory. The leaves on the bushes have burst from their buds. The mosquitoes, awakened, have risen from the damp earth in starving clouds. That man can't feel on his face the hundreds of little stings thirsty for blood. His skin seems to be made of wood. The sun shines down on the forest. The light is heavy on his shoulders, like a sack. Sweat runs down his face, where it blends with spruce resin and soil. He is silent too. He works as fiercely and patiently as a horse. She would run away in fear from this black man if she didn't have to wait and bestow his death. And yet, once she blushed in his presence, timidly. She watches him struggle. She hopes he didn't see her blush. If he did notice, he must have forgotten by now, because he forgets everything. When he has been overwhelmed and he feels death rising from his belly to his head, when he realizes that she has deposited the seed of death in his belly and he beseeches heaven with eyes like the eyes of the child in the snow, she will not blush when he lies dying at her feet. He calls to her. She obeys like a women who does not intend to kill her man. Another stump to uproot. If the horse hadn't been lost in the storm as well ... The man gives orders. Would he speak the same way to the horse? He's eager now. As if he were going to live long enough to harvest. The stumps that cling to the earth with all their roots must be pulled out. Without a horse. Without an ox. Victor drives a young maple trunk under the stump; under the trunk he rolls a log that will serve as a support, then he grasps the top of the trunk. He calls his wife to help him and the two of them, like two beasts of burden, under a cloud of mosquitoes in the heavy light, pull and haul to lower the lever to the ground and pull up the stump whose tentacles creep and cling beneath the earth. At the end of their lever, Virginie and the man must make themselves heavier and stronger than the stump, which has borne a tree and its branches over the winds and seasons of a hundred years. The maple bends. They pull even harder; they press down: the stump has moved. The stump is not as strong as their four arms trembling with the effort, their two bodies trying to weigh more than their weight, the brace of their four legs. Suddenly the earth rips open and the stump seems like a great dead beast pulled from its lair. The man is victorious. He is proud, he smiles. Virginie is silent and submissive as she walks toward another stump. That man starts talking again as soon as he gets his breath back. Virginie doesn't listen; what does the fine, rich soil matter, or fallow land or fields filled with wheat and animals, or seeding and harvesting, what does all that matter to a man who is going to die and the woman who will bestow his death?

*   *   *   *   *

At the end of Lent Christ's painful agony was over; He had died, and then was resurrected on Easter day. The sins of mankind had been expiated. Repentance was no longer necessary. Virginie's parents gave her permission to go out with her friends on Sunday afternoon. In a group, like a bouquet of fresh flowers, they minced toward the Place du Marché. They laughed at the boys they met, who always seemed to one of them ridiculous or old-fashioned, but they would blush if a boy looked up at them. Once he had passed they would start chirping again, maintaining that they'd felt no sudden shivers. Sometimes the boy wore the uniform of the militia. Then Virginie's legs would turn to jelly. She couldn't follow her friends then. She thought she'd caught a glimpse of the soldier who had held her in his arms so long, the night of Mardi Gras. The soldier approached. It wasn't hers. The young man walked past and Virginie's cheeks were redder than her friends'. She became impatient when they laughed at her. "She sees him at every street corner, but he only exists in her head!" She wanted to run away to escape their teasing, but she struggled to feign indifference. "The militiamen court girls the way they fight a war, but boys from offices know how to talk to them," she said, though she didn't believe her own words. One Sunday when she opened the door there was a stranger in the house. She saw, in the rocking chair, the back of a man who was talking to her father and who wasn't rocking. Her mother had taught her good manners: she must greet the visitor, then withdraw without disturbing the adults' conversation. And so she approached the visitor who, sensing her arrival, stopped talking and got to his feet; Virginie ran to her room without uttering a word. Her soldier was in the house! When Virginie's parents saw the robust young man, a soldier who had travelled through forests, blush at the sight of their daughter, they exchanged a glance and smiled. The visitor had no need to explain, to deploy all the precautions he had been taking since he arrived, nor to set out on the complicated detours he was imposing on his story. He began speaking simply. In her room, Virginie had collapsed across the bed. The space between the front door and her room had seemed impassable to her trembling legs. Her heart was pounding as if it wanted to escape from her too slight chest. The sound of her heart reverberated in her head. The visitor, on the other side of the wall, seemed as unreal to her as the militiamen she had seen on the city streets who were never *her* militiaman. She had never doubted that one day she would see him again. And now he was sitting in her own house. She listened to his powerful voice, the voice of a man who sounded older than he looked. It was more like a father's voice than a young man's. Virginie couldn't believe the reality: he was there, in her own house, sitting in the chair where she had often rocked, his boots on the floor her hands had polished. And that voice, her soldier's voice was creeping into her very bedroom, into her bed: "A man's not blessed with the luck to go on such an expedition many times in his life, mon cher monsieur; the soldier's trade has given me the chance, mon cher monsieur, to visit the country far from the city of Quebec. I've travelled sometimes as far as canoes could take us, mon cher monsieur, to where the rivers end. Sometimes we walked in dense forest, to where the trees were squeezed too close together to let a man through sideways, mon cher monsieur. I've gone on foot to the ends of a fair number of roads in this country; so you see, mon cher monsieur, I've had the chance to get to know the country. And if I tell someone, This is the finest piece of land around, that person isn't obliged to believe me; but if he hasn't travelled as much as me, well then I'm not obliged to let him contradict me either. I tell you, mon cher monsieur, I've found the finest spot in this country, and since there's nothing built there yet, I've decided, mon cher monsieur, to build myself a cabin. I'm going to buy the land, I'm going to put my name on it, mon cher monsieur, I'm going to clear it, and that's where I want to live out my life. Where I want to place my descendants too. There's lots of stones in the ground, mon cher monsieur, but it's where I want to live: there's as many spruce trees as a man might want to cut; there's as many mountains as a man might want to cross. It's in that forest, mon cher monsieur, that I want to cut the wood to build my house and barn. It's in that forest, mon cher monsieur, that I want to carve out my man's road. I assure you, mon cher monsieur, that the sky above is so beautiful, when my time comes I want to be buried in that land. That land, mon cher monsieur, needs men. Sowing children in that land will give us a tough race; that land, mon cher monsieur, is rocky and rough and covered with brush. There's swamps; it's steep. It's a land, mon cher monsieur, for a man who loves life when life is hard. When a man gets a look at that land, mon cher monsieur, he loses the urge to go any farther: he'll stop and build a cabin with the spruce trees he'll fell around him, he'll chink it with moss, he'll peel birches to cover the walls and the roof, and once he's taken possession of the territory, he'll record it all in the official papers. If there was any finer place on earth to live, mon cher monsieur, I wouldn't have come to tell you all that; I'd still be looking for it. But the good Lord took me by the hand. You see, mon cher monsieur, holding a rifle isn't enough for a man that the good Lord created and put on this earth, when He could just as well not have created him and put him on this earth. A man must cultivate his land and make children. A man can do other things besides cultivate the land and make children. A man can do other things besides cultivate the land, but if the land isn't cultivated, mon cher monsieur, no man can live. Man's an animal that eats, mon cher monsieur, and if the land isn't cultivated he'll eat his fellow-man. Me, I come from a place where they cultivate the land. It's the only thing I know how to do. I ran away from my father's house; I went to shoot rifles all over Lower Canada because it seems, mon cher monsieur, that the sound of a rifle in peacetime can make people afraid of war. Man's fate is written by the hand of God, mon cher monsieur, and my fate is to go back and cultivate the land. Two days after Mardi Gras this year, I took part in the military demonstration on the Place du Marché; afterwards I asked for my discharge and I went back to my village, where my family's been cultivating the land for three generations. There I found out they were looking for men to accompany a group of monks who were going to build a monastery way up by the mountains, in the forest, beyond Lac Etchemin. There's no road, mon cher monsieur, and no paths, but there's swamps and hillocks and branches as sharp as thorns and as tight as if they were woven together. And mosquitoes!

More than there's lice on a poor scoundrel's head. They're starving, those mosquitoes: even more than the poor scoundrel himself, mon cher monsieur. The men were saying, They're crazy, those monks! I pray the good Lord will forgive us. We couldn't know, mon cher monsieur, that they were inspired by the good Lord. The good Lord's hand had guided them. And my estate, mon cher monsieur, isn't far from where the monastery will be built. The good Lord will scatter blessings on the monastery, like wholesome seed; some of them are bound to be blown by the wind and come to rest on my land and my cabin. Ah, mon cher monsieur! the good Lord's hand showed us the road through a forest, but it didn't trace the road! All the baggage, mon cher monsieur, was transported on the backs of men. A man who's lived the life of the militia can do that without blaspheming too much, even if he's up to his waist in a swamp. Every step, mon cher monsieur, has been gained by the blow of an axe. To take a step, we often had to fell a tree. At the end of the road there'll be a monastery for men of God, and there'll be a new village. As men make their way through the country, the wild animals move back. The good Lord's given me life; He's given me some fine land where I want to live the life He's given me. Life and some land—that's two generous gifts from the Lord. Now if you, mon cher monsieur, would be agreeable to granting me the hand of your daughter, Mademoiselle Virginie, that would make three precious gifts. I'd take real good care of her. I won't have a castle to shelter her, only a log cabin. The good Lord will love your daughter and me, mon cher monsieur, and later on I could give her a house. That's what I wanted to tell you, mon cher monsieur, and that's why I came here. I've talked long enough; now you know all my weak points. If the good Lord gave me any qualities, you've spotted them too, and you know if you want me for a son-in-law. Mon cher monsieur, if you do want me for a son-in-law, and if the good Lord intended me to protect Mademoiselle Virginie, the marriage could take place the first week in June: that's a good season for weddings. I wouldn't take her from you right away; after the marriage I'd leave her with you. I'd go back to my land and clear it and prepare for my wife to join me under my roof. I'd work all summer and the next autumn and winter, then I'd return around the end of March to bring her back with me. And by then, if the good Lord's willing, she might be carrying a baby in her arms."

* * * * *

I nstead of straining to turn the earth with a pick, instead of wrenching his arms as he shreds the unyielding peat, instead of sweating for days and days as he raises his pick, which grows heavier each time, instead of hurling insults at the good Lord into the sky when his pick strikes a stone or gets caught in the tenacious roots of sedge and alder that have been tangled together since the beginning of time, instead of persisting in doing the work of a beast while suffering like a man, why doesn't that man go to the monastery and borrow an ox and cart? He won't borrow anything from the monks; if he didn't have his pick, that man would plough with his fingers and nails, and if he didn't have hands, rather than go and ask for help he would chew the earth with his teeth. Borrow an ox and a cart from the monks? He doesn't want to be judged yet again. He doesn't want to be judged because he's already forgotten that snowstorm. He has forgotten the child. That man, who thinks only of harvests, has no memory. What he has forgotten doesn't exist. The good monks are fair; they know how the man has sinned against life. Can such a man avoid the curse of God who, in His wisdom, must be sorry He created a man who can't maintain the life that He bestowed on a child? He didn't want to confess to the monks, who would have erased his sin. He wanted to erase it himself, by forgetting. He has not returned to the monastery since the night of the catastrophe. He has too much work to do, he says. He doesn't want to meet those who have a memory. So he ploughs the land with a pick. He is alone against the land. He will be alone until the day when the land inflicts a just punishment on him. He will be alone when he dies. He is even more alone because he is with a woman who does not forgive him. Often the land retains the pick. It takes a hard struggle to wrench it out; he exerts himself as if the child were still alive; he tackles the land as if it did not contain his child; he works as if he had not killed. Inside the cabin, Virginie prepares wild garlic. She learned about the plant, which is both bitter and sweet, from that man: in the militia, he came upon it during long marches through the forest. "This plant's not poisonous, Virginie, it's one of the good Lord's pleasant gifts." He knows that she is going to do away with herself. She hasn't spoken to him since the catastrophe. Such silence can conceal only death, he has to admit it. Why should the mother speak when the child will be silent until the end of the world? Why should the mother speak to the man who cast her child into silence? Did he resemble that man? A child's eyes change. She doesn't remember. She doesn't remember the sound of his voice, or the sound of his cries in the house at night; he seemed to be calling for help. Was he, already, terrorized by the dreadful night in which he would soon disappear? She wanted to hold him in her arms, let him drink as he clung, quivering, to her breast. Her milk was the blood of this restless little heart that, without her, would have been unable to beat. She gave her milk and she was happy. Her heart was beating too, in his thirsty little heart. She was happy. The good Lord had created her and put her on earth so she could hold this child in her arms and feed him her milk that would keep him alive. She had been created to safeguard the life of this child. The good Lord had given the child life, but it was her task to perpetuate it. She must go with him until he parted from her to enter the world of men. She'd been born for this child who had come from her womb. Carrying her baby in her arms she walked on the streets of Quebec like a queen. She no longer blushed when a man looked at her. She knew something he could never know, knowledge accessible only to mothers. Her body had never known such pride. The pride of being young and pretty seemed insipid, now that she knew the honor of carrying in the winter light a child that had come from her womb. She had borne him, not since the day when a man had placed his seed in her, but since the far-off day when her mother had taught her that little girls, like fruits, when they are grown and when the season is right, give life to babies, while boys have strong arms to do exhausting work that makes them snore dully at night. She had dreamed so often of that child in her arms, she had been waiting so long for him that the child was almost her age. She would teach him everything she had learned since the time when she was as small as he; she thought of that when she walked on the street, not so she'd be noticed by young men now, who felt nuptial fever rising in them, but to expose her child to the country's air, let him breathe the air from the river that gives its might to the men of the land of Quebec. Today, Virginie's fingers, chafed by the edges of stones she has gathered, are burned by the wild garlic; she takes pains with her task. She is dreaming of a warm little weight in the hollow of her belly. Really, her belly must remember the child's presence. She wipes her hands and touches her belly through the cloth. She caresses a memory. She leaves her hand there for a long time. Her belly remembers nothing. When she thinks she remembers, she is succumbing to the disease of lonely people who think they hear noises or imagine they feel pain. She remembers not a child, but a gust of wind blowing over their life. In the middle of the forest, where the wind carries the distant sounds of hammers and axes, and of logs thrown one on top of the other to build the monastery, Virginie is alone as she will be when she is put in chains for having carried out on earth the justice God has already rendered in Heaven: alone as a mother who has lost her child. She imagines memories. She does not even remember the rending of her body when the child was born. She wishes she could remember the pain; that would retrieve, a little, the life of her child. She sees only the snow that fell upon the land and upon a woman's cries. That man is coming home: she hears his footsteps; the brush cracks under his feet. In the winter, because of the snow, she only heard him when he was singing one of the songs he'd learned in the militia, that echoed coarse words as if there were no God in Heaven to hear them. Now that it's summer, he crushes everything he steps on. Her hands peel the wild garlic. He is going to push the door: she hears his footsteps at the door. He stops: what does he hear as he stands there? His shoulder rubs against the door. He must be watching some small animal he's caught sight of. Perhaps he's sniffing the partridge that's roasting in the stove. Perhaps he's getting ready to explain to her yet again why they should make a child. More cracking sounds. He's started walking again. His shoulder rubs again against the birchbark that lines the cabin. He's breathing hard. He's been running. Why is he bent over? Has he seen an animal digging under the wall? He pants as if he's been running. Why doesn't he speak? That man transforms life into words. Why is he silent now? She doesn't look up. She knows he's looking in the window. During the day they lift the cloth from the opening that's been cut in the wall. Why is the man spying on her through the pane like a jailer? He is clutching the wood: she hears him scratch the wood as if he had claws.

Claws? She looks up. A bear. Its head is in the opening. It almost fills the cabin. Before she can move, she screams. Red sparks glow in the bear's eyes. It opens its jaws: its teeth gleam like fire. With its jaws open, the animal's head is even bigger. Virginie screams all her terror, her lungs gripped by fear. The big head turns, first to one side, then the other, the big red mouth searches for prey. The head is so big it could tear off the roof with one convulsive movement. The bear's neck is stuck. This opening is too small to let him in. If he persists, he'll demolish the wall. The logs are already vibrating. He growls with massive pleasure. He sniffs the rich odor of roast partridge. Feeling himself wedged in the windowpane, he panics. He growls. Virginie is pushed backwards by the power of his voice. In the great hairy head the eyes shine very brightly, but he seems not to see. It's excruciating to be looked at by eyes that shine but do not see. The great hairy arms and the claws that gleam like fangs try to grasp what the little red eyes do not see. There is anger in those blind eyes. It is, rather, the animal's jaws that see. His mouth is a big red eye between eyelids of gleaming fangs. Virginie knows no place where she can hide from this mouth that sees her and smells the odour of her woman's body. She flattens herself in the corner. She calls out, she screams to be heard by that man to whom she hasn't said a single word since that catastrophic night. She cries out louder than the silence to which she has condemned the man; she cries as if all the words held in by her silence were welling up because she is going to die. The wall cannot protect her from those blood-streaked jaws, from those blind eyes and the powerful body that is smashing the logs and breaking the joints. That man is spading the earth where he wants to plant his first potatoes, which he says will be ready to boil in August. In August, he won't be there. And where will she be, if the bear knocks down the wall? Her howls are as savage as the growling of the beast. The beast is as hot as a stove. The animal sniffs the smell of her woman's flesh. She

74

screams. Does the man hear her call, or is he as deaf as he was one snowy, windy night? Her call is a cry. She cries out to frighten the ferocious beast that is tearing down the cabin wall. With a crack, the roof falls in. She will be imprisoned with the bear, crushed by the fallen roof and the caved-in walls. She screams. Will that man come and save her life? If God wants justice to be done, He will order the man who is peacefully spading the soil to come and save the life of the woman who is to punish him with death. She does not want to die now. She will be punished when she has rendered justice to the man, but she does not want to be tortured before justice has been done. She doesn't want to be tormented by the black animal's red mouth. She screams, she implores the man whom she must kill, to save her life. When the animal opens its mouth, the smell of rotten food in its stomach springs to her face. The woman exists now only through her cries. The bear growls, then suddenly it has stopped growling and is moaning and crying; convulsive movements shake its great fur-wrapped body. The huge head with gleaming eyes is no longer trying to enter the cabin. The beast is in contortions, trying to wrench itself from the window. She backs away. The wall and the roof are tangled together. Virginie hears the voice of the man, but she stays in the corner, transfixed, as if the huge beast were still threatening her. She hears shouting, abuse. The man has come to her rescue; he rails against the animal. She hears him blaspheme. Her body swaying on legs numb with fear, she staggers to the window. The bear's black fur is stained with blood. The bear stands erect, gigantic, and the man is attacking the wild beast with a spade. He strikes. Blood gushes. The beast moans. He hurls abuse and strikes again. The beast brings down its powerful foot. He strikes and blasphemes. There is blood on him. Is he wounded? He cries out. Is he addressing the animal or her? He strikes. The spade sinks into the fur and the fat flesh opens, bleeding. The bear growls. He calls to all the bears in the forest for help. The man's knees give way. He crumples to the ground. The beast dares not advance for the spade is still threatening; erect, it gets down on all fours again. Its groans come not from suffering now, but fury. The bear walks around the prostrate man. He is no longer threatened. He seeks a place to attack without being struck by the spade. He is bleeding. His fur is more red than black, but he doesn't care: he will kill this vanquished enemy lying on the ground. Will God's justice be rendered by a savage beast? Virginie could leave the bear to punish the man with death. Then she would go to the monastery and tell how the man was killed by a bear, and the monks, in little whispering voices, would explain that God in His wisdom had decided that the man must be killed by a bear; they would explain that things which occur on earth may seem mysterious to humans, but that everything happens through the will of God, who is wisdom and justice. If the bear puts that man to death no one will condemn her, like the Lady, to wear chains at her ankles. Virginie has never touched a rifle. The rifle stands in the corner, always loaded. She seizes it, looks for the place where she must insert her finger and press; she goes outside. The bear has decided to attack the head of the man, who can't stand up but is brandishing a spade. Virginie approaches. The bear isn't worried about her. His mouth is open. His jaws have measured the man's skull. Virginie, utterly fearless, touches the animal with her rifle. He growls. Virginie steps back and pulls the trigger: hot blood spatters her face. A thunderous roar echoes in the forest. The beast comes crashing down. She is seized by a profound desire to speak. She turns her back on the fallen man and beast. She is silent. Throwing down the rifle, she goes inside the cabin.

*　　*　　*　　*　　*

Why didn't Virginie abandon the man to the ferocious beast? Why is she urged on by death like a bud towards its leaf? What does she understand? When her story is told on nights in years to come, people will remember only the sound of chains at her ankles. They will understand no more than she does. And the forest all around, as vast as a silent woman's solitude; the forest of which she sees only the verge around the cabin, but which stretches out like a sea! It would take only one small convulsion, a few waves, and the cabin would be covered with rolling branches, green and black, it would cave in amid whirling shadows and needles and bark. Even if she were a bird that could climb into the sky, she couldn't see the full expanse of the forest. It is so vast, she's been told, that it overflows into other countries. What more will come out of this forest? In the winter, starving animals come and prowl around the cabin in the night. They prowl in Virginie's dreams as well. How many bears are still in the forest, sniffing the cabin's odor of simmering meat? As soon as the snow had melted the forest released its mosquitoes. They swooped down in black clouds. Driven, they crept in every-where. It would be impossible to live in the cabin they invaded if it weren't worse outside. They attack, they harpoon, they sting. Cloth doesn't resist them. They chew with their little fangs, their pointed lips burrow deep in the flesh, to drink the blood; they prick nerves, they enter ears, they spur eardrums and beat their wings inside the head. They get trapped in hair, they struggle and sting and bite. When the drop of blood wells up they bathe in it. Mosquitoes hum, bite, bombard, they search for blood in the nostrils. Nothing drives them away: neither blows nor the dense smoke given off when grass and moss are thrown on the fire, nor the camphor that Virginie wears in a pouch around her neck. If men could read God's signs, that man would realize that the mosquitoes are forbidding him to go deeper into the forest. But he persists. The mosquitoes torment day and night. The nights are sleepless and longer than the harrowing days. The mosquitoes turn the air into sharp bushes. And what will the forest hurl at them next? Wasn't the Lady who accompanies her born of the forest too? In her childhood, Virginie had heard the Lady's story; certain episodes, in which you could hear the sound of chains, reminded her of certain winter nights before the fire, when the wind was blowing hard against the stone walls. For days and nights, and then more days and nights, in her closed cabin, surrounded by snow that piled higher and higher, she listened to the wind in the forest. When she had listened for a long time she realized that the wind was not a breath but a voice, that it wasn't blowing, but singing, and its song was a lament. And in the sorrow of its song she began to recognize old tunes; the wind was so sorrowful it recalled dead songs. During long nights when sleep refused to take her to the black land where people die, then are resurrected at dawn in the light, she listened to the wind. Beside her that man slept and snored like an exhausted horse. But she stayed awake. Listening to the forest's song she heard once more the melodies of childhood, stories told before the fire by old people who seemed to know only the past. At night, dead souls roam, singing softly, compliantly, between the forest's trunks and branches. The soul of the Lady had entered her body like a song of a departed voice. God had breathed upon the earth and given it a soul, and then Adam appeared. And thus in the wind of the forest Virginie was born, a new woman, unknown to herself; her new soul came from the forest, where the trees breathe, where you can hear the strength of the earth rise from the ground into treetrunks, where past mysteries awaken under thick moss and rotted leaves, where dead stories come back to life and where beasts kill in order to live. Her new soul is vast and unknown, like the forest around her: it is she who must kill that man. The bear has already come to bring him death, but she saved him. She has prevented God's justice from being fulfilled. And yet, she wants only that justice. She wants to render it herself. She is silent, as unfathomable as the forest where so many departed voices roam.

*   *   *   *   *

When the bear has fallen, struck by the rifle's thunder, his big paw drops heavily onto Victor's chest but does not tear it. The big head and its muzzle fall onto his shoulder; the bear is still roaring, but cannot bite, and Victor, for whom talking is breathing, remains silent. Silently, as in church, with rather solemn piety, he sinks his pick in the animal's neck. Without uttering a word he watches the blood gush from the neck and soak the earth, which becomes red mud. Then, still not speaking, when all of the animal's blood has drained, he bends over it and, briskly wielding his knife, starts cutting the skin from the belly. He spreads open the fur. The bear's big belly bursts out in strips. Virginie doesn't look. The man bending over the bear he is skinning now seems as big as the bear that has crashed to the ground. As long as they've lived in the forest he hasn't stopped growing; he is stronger and stronger, as if some sap had been beneficial to his body. He wasn't afraid to attack a bear with his pick. Perhaps he would have slain the wild animal if she hadn't fired the rifle. Has the soul of the trees entered her body? Could the strength of unknown things behind the trees have entered her soul? For her, the sound of the forest is repeating the stories of catastrophes. Is it possible that the same forest voice murmurs to this man the story of future harvests? She doesn't understand. There are so many things she doesn't understand. But doesn't being a woman mean not understanding? That man bent over the dead beast resembles the forest where he dwells. That man, who one night crossed through the land of death, knows nothing but life. He is rooted among the trees; he is part of a life that engenders life as the forest engenders the forest, with the same constant force. She cannot leave the land of death which she entered with this man, one night when a storm was raging. She and he no longer inhabit the same country. In hers, chains ring out on the Lady's ankles. She will not come back to life until she has killed that man who dragged her onto the black road of death. She hears him striking with his axe. The sound is the sound of blows hitting a rotted trunk. At times the axe makes a dry sound, as on a young maple: she realizes he is chopping the great beast to pieces: in the blazing sun the disembowelled body, bleeding and bare, has already started to rot. It smells bad, as it did when the beast stuck its head in the window. When the man is laid out on the ground, when the sun cooks his body, will his death smell like the bear's? She doesn't want to see him; and yet she has gone back to the opening in the wall. On his shoulder he carries something that looks like a big branch: an animal's paw. It seems very heavy. He walks toward the trees, at the end of the space he has cleared. His clothes are soaked in blood. He walks in a cloud of blackflies. That dead meat will attract carnivorous animals: it must be buried far from the house. She observes him at length. He carries all the hard pieces into the forest, with the exception of a piece of thigh which he fastens to a branch above the ground. He shoves the soft and sticky pieces into a cloth bag—the guts, the bowels, the stomach—and several times he will empty the bag behind the trees. When everything is clean, except for the blood that is soaking into the ground, he rolls up the bear's skin and she sees him walking, bowed down by his black-and-red burden. Will he bury the fur as well? Will he wash off the dried blood in the stream? At sunset, he emerges from the forest, the bear's skin over his head and outstretched arms. The beast that she killed is alive again. She will kill that man who is dressed in the fur of a savage beast.

*　*　*　*　*

81

"**D**id you see them this morning, Virginie, on top of the furrows, did you see the little shoots? What a fine sight! It's starting! Our real life coming out of the earth: the first shoots! They'll grow, Virginie! We've sown; the earth will return to us a hundredfold what we've given it. Just think—outside your door there'll be a vegetable garden. When you go out of the cabin you'll take a few steps, just a few steps, and there at your feet, Virginie, at your feet, there'll be potatoes as fine as you've ever seen at the market in Quebec, new potatoes that the rich folks from the Upper Town can't afford to buy, and later we'll have carrots and beets. Maybe I'll be able to buy butter if I sell my wood to the monastery and if the monks will pay for it. Virginie, I'm going to ask you a favor .... I'm a man who blushes, I can't sell a thing. If I give my wood away, then I can't buy butter. Maybe the holy monks won't want to live in a monastery made from wood cut by the hands of a man the good Lord singled out for misfortune. I'm a proud man, and if I take my wood to the monks and I see a glint in their eyes accusing me of that catastrophe that happened to us .... You know, Virginie, it's the good Lord Himself, in that snow as thick and black as if the whole world had burned up, it's the good Lord Himself who wanted a child to be sacrificed to Him, just like in the Bible when He asked Abraham to offer up the life of his beloved son; me, I'm not a holy man like Abraham, I haven't heard the good Lord's voice, but I've felt His hand on me, crushing me; Virginie, the good Lord didn't ask us to build a funeral pyre, like Abraham, but He created a storm like I've never seen, so our child would be sacrificed to Him . . . . Virginie, I'm a proud man. To be worthy of living, you have to be proud, prouder than death. If one of the monks lets me see—me, already feeling like a beggar because I must offer my wood—just a glint of reproach in his eye, I couldn't bear the humiliation. If I can attack a bear, I don't know what I could do to a monk in his habit. I'm paralyzed at the thought of it and I can't take a step toward the monastery. Virginie, it's the finest spruce, tall and straight, that the good Lord seems to have cultivated specially to make fine walls without knots, for the monks in His monastery, fine spruce that I've squared off well. Virginie, I'm giving you this spruce: it's yours. The monks have no reason to humiliate you. The monks can't criticize you for being a victim the good Lord singled out. Virginie, I'm asking you a favor like the day I asked your father for the favor of according me your hand: go and sell the monks the spruce that I've felled . . . . And if we sell some wood to the sawmill too, I may be able to buy a cow to replace the one the good Lord took from us . . . . We'll have everything a man and a woman could hope for on earth: a roof, a fire in the hearth, food, wood to sell and land where we're king and queen . . . . But Virginie, we're alone. Me, I'm not alone because you're there, but you, Virginie, you're alone with our catastrophe. And if you're alone, well then, so am I: I'm just as alone as you are . . . . The big storm is over: the snow's gone. It's summer. June. We must forget the winter, Virginie. All the trees around us have forgotten the winter. If the good Lord has put a memory in men's souls, it's as much for forgetting as remembering. If men always remembered everything, they'd be the unhappiest creatures in God's creation. We've suffered as much as a catastrophe can make a man and woman suffer. You, you suffer and you're silent; me, I suffer and I talk as if I felt no pain. We mustn't turn our backs on this summer that the good Lord's sending us as a blessing, all bright with sun and filled with miracles. We're alone, you and me, alone in the midst of an earthly paradise, living as if it wasn't summer; and I'm telling you it's wrong to refuse God's beautiful summer. This beautiful summer, Virginie, is the good Lord's way of talking to us, and when He talks to us, He's telling us to live, because summer is life. It's a sin, Virginie, not to see the miracles God makes for us. You and me, we must obey the summer the good Lord's giving us. In the summer everything that's alive yields its fruit; this summer our land will give us its fruits and vegetables. And man and woman must bear their fruits too, Virginie. We mustn't stay here alone like dry trees. We mustn't stay alone. The monks don't make children but you and me, we aren't monks. If all men were monks, who'd make the children who become monks? We've started to conquer a new land, and that land is asking for men and women. Virginie, we must give it children. You mustn't decide on your own that you're a barren apple-tree. You're full of life and you must pass on that life. Only the good Lord can decide if an apple tree's barren or fertile. If it's fertile, it's because the good Lord has blessed it; if it's barren, the good Lord has cursed it; Virginie, the good Lord doesn't want to curse you. When I see the black silence around us, I ask myself if some other catastrophe isn't waiting to strike. Virginie, if you'd say just one word.... Speech is a gift from God, Virginie. You don't have the right to refuse the good Lord's gift. He gave you speech and He gave you life, Virginie. You have no right to live as if He'd given you silence and death."

*   *   *   *   *

She ought to love that man. He has righted the wall of the cabin. Outside the window he has planted posts, tapered at the top and sharply pointed; that way, any curious animal would hurt itself before it reached the window. He has stretched the bear's skin over a frame that he made from four birch trees. Every day he stretches the skin a little more. "Next winter, Virginie, you won't be cold in your bed," he says; "I promise you'll never be cold. You'll be protected from the winter cold like a bear." Next winter he won't be with her to worry about whether she's cold; he won't even know what season it is on the earth. That man has all the qualities of a man who is loved. If she were still a girl who hadn't seen a child come out of her womb, whose ideas had got tangled up when a man walked by, like her hair when a gust of wind blew off the river, she'd still enjoy dancing with him, dancing for a long time, even though he no longer wears a militiaman's clothes and even though he has the wrinkled face of someone who knows a lot. Since he has been battling the forest, he will never again be able to look like a young man who enjoys dancing. Now he is a man who works. Even in the most exuberant dance, when the fiddles invented the wildest, most extravagant music, the stress of work could never be erased from his face. If she were still the girl who had danced so late with him on the night of Mardi Gras, who was only music, whirling faster than the earth, she would agree to dance again with that man. He seems not to know the past, to remember only the future. She has heard him; she knows he hasn't forgotten that winter night when a child would die. She knows now: he doesn't think only of what could be born, he thinks also of what has died. If she were still a girl, she would dance with that man whose face is always a little sad because he has forgotten nothing. The music would seem to her as happy as it did that night when the chaperone had to tear her away from the dancing; then, there was no memory, there was no tomorrow. She would be able to lean against his chest and enjoy feeling him as solid as a firmly rooted maple. She will put him to death when the time comes. She is no longer that girl, she is no longer the young woman who saw the child come out of her womb, she is no longer the mother of that child who drank at her breast and whom the man looked at, prophesying that he would drink his life just as avidly. She is someone else. Someone else inhabits her body. Her soul died with the child. In the stories they used to tell at evening gatherings and on nights when the wind blew hard, she could hear chains dragging in the night. Could it be that the Lady from the distant land of France, on the other side of the sea, is an ancestor who has given her blood to Virginie's body and now is handing on her wandering soul? She can no longer love that man. Already the chains ring out at her ankles.

*　*　*　*　*

They had been gone from Quebec for three days now. They reached the end of the road. They stopped for the night at the last house before the forest. The child had been crying constantly and had refused to drink. The farmers agreed to give them shelter; they brought in the horse and the cow, steaming from walking all day long in snow that sucked them in like white mud. On this winter day the animals were sweating as if it were summer. They stowed the sleigh under the stairs in the stable. The woman showed Virginie and the child into a house that smelled of cabbage soup. The man put a canvas cover over the sleigh, after he had diligently taken an inventory of its contents: the barrel of salt pork, the sacks of potatoes and flour, the boxes of biscuits, the tea, molasses and maize. It was night. The man had wanted to keep going as late as possible. He had persisted, even though the horse was so exhausted its knees were quaking like a drunken man's. Victor said that the later they travelled that day, the sooner they would reach the cabin the day after. After supper, the women talked about children's illnesses. The farmer's wife had had eight, two of whom were dead; she was pregnant, she knew about children. "Your child," she said, "doesn't have a hot forehead or a cold belly, so he's not sick, but he's crying so hard, I tell you he must be very frightened. See, he's looking at you and doesn't even recognize you, his own mother! He must be very frightened not to recognize his mother. I tell you, that child's had a big fright. Even though he's in your arms, his mother's arms, that child is crying for help. Children know many things. Before they're born, you know, they kick your belly, their own mother's. Why? They know that they're going to be born. I tell you, children know the future. The good Lord came and took our last two, to be angels in Heaven. Well now! Those two didn't want to go: I tell you, they cried as hard as yours. You're a mother too! You know how a mother's heart would suffer if she heard her two babies crying because they didn't want to go back to paradise, where they came from. Oh, it's sad, but didn't the good Lord make mothers to carry children in their bellies—and to bear men's suffering on their shoulders? If your child's crying hard enough to tear open his chest, it's because he's scared; he feels the forest all around him, he hears the branches moving like great hairy arms. It's enough to scare anyone. You're a mother; now admit it, you're afraid of the forest too. That infant can't eat unless you feed him. He can't walk, except in your arms. He's afraid of those trees that are so much taller than he is. He doesn't know where you're taking him, but he senses you're taking him very far. He's afraid of getting lost. He's afraid you'll abandon him in the forest. And he's crying. He's scared. You're a mother and you're scared too, scared of getting lost, scared your man will turn into a wild animal in the forest and abandon you or devour you with his teeth. You're scared of the cabin that's waiting for you. A child can't be any less scared than his mother. When my two little angels went up to the good Lord's Heaven, screaming as if they were going to Hell, they cried because they were scared. Me too, I'm scared of death, and so are you, because you're a mother. But your fear doesn't make you cry hard enough to vomit your lungs: no, you hold your child tighter, you clutch that frail little man, you hold him against your breasts. And you say nothing. That's how mothers are: they suffer their children's suffering." The men were smoking and talking as if they couldn't hear the crying child. They talked about clearing the land; they talked about a sawmill that soon would be built; then they wouldn't have to square off trunks with an axe or saw them into planks with a two-handed saw. Their host talked about how you could make potash from wood-ashes, by leaving them to soak in water for a month, then boiling them in a big kettle. "Potash is good for nothing but making soap, but there's a lot of demand for it in the City of Quebec, where you can sell it. Apparently they ship it overseas." A man from the village had burned his potash in a stone oven; it produced better potash and he sold it for a small fortune. They talked about lime, which you shouldn't buy but make yourself, by burning limestone to ashes. ("The good Lord thought of everything. He knew men would need all sorts of things: the good Lord's like the owner of a general store where you can find everything a man needs.") The child howled out his fear to the night, which had fallen, weighty and starless, over the farmer's house. They talked about the distance they still had to travel in the forest, about the mosquitoes the previous summer that had prevented the men from cutting a road through the forest; they talked about how lucky he was to be clearing his land, as they said, in a parish where there were monks to pray for the inhabitants all day and all night. They assessed the hardness of the snow, to determine if it could support the sleigh. They were afraid the sun's warmth had spoiled the snow: it could slip away under the sleigh like rotten wood; they convinced each other how important it was for the man not to command the horse in this dangerous snow, but to obey it. They appraised the cow's astonishing ability to move, even though her udder was dragging in the snow. They cursed the wolves that approached the road. The farmer said that if he had his life to live over, he'd start again beside the spot where Victor had built his cabin: "The trees are good, they grow up thick and fast, like weeds; the mountains are high and a man on a mountain is closer to Heaven and the good Lord is closer to man." Then the farmer threw some logs into the stove; the woman offered Virginie some holy water, for their prayers. It was time for bed. At dawn, she still hadn't slept. The child hadn't stopped crying. The men carried the sacks out to the sleigh, harnessed the horse, and fastened the cow in back while Victor, beaming, reined his horse:

"May the good Lord take care of you like you took care of us and our animals!"

"Ask the monks to pray the good Lord will spread sunshine over our land!"

"We don't ask Him for wealth; but we're glad when He watches us, like He watches His little birds!"

The sun rose; when it had set, the horse would be in his shelter beside the cow; he'd have had his oats and she would be chewing her hay. A fire would be burning in the hearth. When he had left the cabin to go and get his wife and child in the city of Quebec, the man had been careful to stack some dry wood in the stove to light the first fire when they arrived at the cabin. Suddenly the child stopped crying. "He's not afraid now," Virginie said. "That child will be sorry for the rest of his life that he can't remember this journey," said Victor.

*   *   *   *   *

T he snow was soft. Weighted down by the sacks, the plough, the axes, the two-handed saw, the traps, the frame saw, the handsaws and the sewing machine, the sleigh glided over the snow as if it were water. The cow followed silently, its great eyes submissive. Patiently, the horse clove the snow with his chest. The March sun hadn't touched it. Neither the sun nor the mildest March winds had entered between the tall cliffs of tight-packed spruce. The forest shadows held sway. The snow was blue. The silence was frozen. At times a dry branch would fall, bringing with it a brief avalanche. The breathing of the foundering animals seemed huge in the silence. There was also the clicking of iron fittings on the shafts. The animals trampled bushes with their feet. The sleigh glided along. Suddenly it pitched, lifted by a sudden wave. The horse's chest strained in the harness, then the sleigh straightened out, creaking and cracking. Fine snow was starting to fly. Was it falling from the spruce trees? Was it being churned up by the wind? Was it snow from the sky? The man searched the sky, which was not blue now, but grey. The swirling, dancing snow already veiled the spruce trees. Virginie listened to the hissing of the sleigh runners: she might have thought she was hearing the sound of passing time. The man tried to get a glimpse of the sky. "Smells like a storm." The snow, much thicker now, clung to faces and eyes. When she was coming out of the church, her wedding veil had stuck to her face; blinded, to keep from falling, she had clutched her husband's arm. The snow lashed their faces.

Closed eyelids protected their eyes. Virginie pulled the blanket up to the child's face; he did not move. Wrapped snugly in wool, he slept in her arms. She couldn't feel him breathing through the thickness of the blankets. His little body was heavy. The snow whipped her face, which felt nothing now. She opened her eyes. The spruce and the sky had turned white. It was as soft as sleep. Her body was prepared to give up, but she struggled, for she was holding against her the small firm weight of her child who had stopped crying; nor was he moving in his woollen blankets. She thought of death, which makes humans and animals motionless. The child was no longer afraid. Had she finally managed to reassure him? Now it was she who feared the silence of the trees surrounding her, though she couldn't see them; thick and violent snow covered heaven and earth. The forest seemed no longer to exist. Or was it they who had ceased to exist? The tall and firmly rooted spruce trees were withstanding the storm; but they, in the sleigh . . . And the child, who was so weak? Why did he not cry out, giving voice to the human fear in this forest? A child, a child's cry would have expressed what adult words could not. A great cry. The sleigh wavered. A bestial moan. The horse had screamed. "It had to happen," the man mumbled, jumping off the sleigh. Groping through the night as if he were blind, sinking down with every step, he saw that they were no longer following the passage cut out through the trees. Where were they? She had never heard him swear. She thought that he didn't insult the good Lord like other men. Even though they were lost in the middle of the forest, in a storm, that man was daring to insult the One who, with a single thought, could make them disappear, they and their horse and their cow and the sleigh laden with all their possessions and the huddled child, so small in his blankets. He could bury them and not leave a trace. The man blasphemed. The sleigh was shaken: the horse, who had fallen on his side, was writhing; he wept, a huge child, he wept, he knew his death was near. "He's broken a leg," the man howled. Was the animal calling his mother, like a man about to die? The helpless animal was sobbing as he lay there, unable to kick, unable to rise; his broken leg tormented him. He didn't want to die and he howled out his suffering to everything that was free of pain. The man took his rifle, then put it back. "No, I must save my bullets." He rummaged among the sacks, then brought out an axe. She saw him disappear ahead of her. Some blows rang out. He had cut off the animal's head with the axe. To Virginie, it seemed that the horse cried a little, then grew silent. Ahead of the sleigh a red stain appeared that the driving snow could not hide. That man came back to the sleigh. "Virginie, we're going to walk to our land, to our cabin, and even though it's late, even though it's night, we'll light a fire in our stove and we'll light a lamp in the window. We're going to spend this night in our cabin, by our stove, where a fire from our own wood will be burning." He decided to abandon everything in the sleigh. They would walk. No doubt they could reach the monastery before nightfall, if they battled wind and snow. They must take the cow, for when the wolves came to devour the horse, their teeth would attack the cow too. Virginie would carry the child. Victor tied the cow's rope around his waist. He took the axe and the rifle, searched in the sacks of potatoes, took a few handfuls of flour which immediately turned doughy in his hands, and gruel to feed the child. Furious snowflakes assailed his eyes like a cloud of enraged mosquitoes. Driven by the blizzard, the snow on the ground rose up like a tide. Never could he walk with so many things on his back, the cow behind him, the rifle and axe in his hands. It was hard simply moving his own body's weight. Soon, no doubt, he would have to help Virginie carry the child. So he tossed what he could into a sack—some potatoes, flour, oatmeal—blaspheming. Virginie told him: "Our child is asleep; I don't want him awakened by his father insulting the good Lord." Victor made the sign of the cross; if he had offended the good Lord it was because the Devil had taken advantage of the storm to worm his way into his body. They tied snowshoes to their feet; they walked around the horse, the huge bloodstain, and set out. She held the child to her breast. He walked ahead of her, pulling the cow. The snow was soft, deep; the ground below was re-absorbed. Their snowshoes sank in. About her ankles, clinging mud closed in around her feet. With a great effort she pulled herself out and moved the heavy snowshoe. She felt her feet being gripped as if a hand were squeezing them. The snow wanted to swallow her, but whenever she thought of giving in, the way you give in to sleep, she would take another step. The snow kept getting deeper, even though she was walking in the steps of the man and the animal. The cold stung her feet. Wasn't their cabin too far away? Going back to the neighboring village was impossible: the farmer's house where they had slept was as far away, the man had said, as their own cabin which awaited them; in the monastery they would be given hot soup and a fire to warm their hands and feet. The wind was not held back now, not by the trees or the cloth of their coats or the sturdy wool. Their skin hardened; Virginie could feel cracks in her cheeks. And the snow on the ground, ever thicker, seemed to advance like a contrary current. As a child, she used to bathe her feet in the river, hiking her skirts up to her knees, and the water would push so hard against her legs, it sometimes tipped her over. Now the snow was pushing against her body, to knock her down. She didn't want them to go any further. Was the good Lord giving them a sign not to proceed in this direction? Was the good Lord forbidding them to go, with the child, to the cabin far from the city of Quebec, in the middle of the forest? Perhaps He didn't want the child to live in the forest. Perhaps He didn't want them to attack the forest He created. Was the storm His whip? She remembered the Lady from the childhood stories that were told on nights filled with high winds and snow. Like the Lady, at each step she was dragging at her ankles long, heavy chains. Her face was burning now. The snow melted on it. From time to time the cow's backbone emerged as if it had drowned in the snow and now was floating. She didn't see her man in the blizzard. She was following. Never would she be able to reach their cabin, never would she get to the monastery. She was walking, but the whole forest was walking with her. With every step she took, the trees took a step. The current of snow seemed to be making her drift in the opposite direction; was it taking her back where she'd come from? She wished she could float on the snow the way she'd seen wood float on the river. Her only desire was to lie on her stomach with her child, then fall asleep and let the current carry her. Suddenly, a sob. She remembered the horse's suffering. The child wasn't hurt because he was in her arms, wrapped in woollen blankets, pressed against her. He was afraid again. The cry sounded very feeble in the midst of a storm that was greater than the forest, but it was a great cry for so small a chest. The fear that had tormented him the night before, then, had been stronger than his sleep. She advanced, laboriously, as if she had been condemned to pull a cart filled with stones. It was her own body that was so heavy. At every step she must break down a wall of snow. Her snowshoes caught on bushes. Debris from the walls collapsed around her body, clasping her tightly. The child was crying. Breathless, with no strength left, sweating, her thick woollen socks wet, she crushed him in her arms so that he wouldn't feel alone in the middle of the storm. Her arms felt only her own chest. the small burden wrapped in blankets was no longer in her arms. She screamed. Immediately, far ahead of her, the man's voice responded. If she had been attacked by wolves there wouldn't have been more anguish in her scream. The man's voice, ahead of her, was reproaching her amid the gusting snow. She was paralyzed. Where was the child? There was nothing now but the vast white forest. There was no road. Suddenly the man loomed up ahead of her, very close, with his sweaty man's smell. She was crying, but he probably didn't see the tears that mingled with the snow which had melted on her face. The man's face was masked in ice. When he asked why she was crying, the mask crazed over. She shuddered. Why fear this man just because ice had fallen from his face? Only he could help her.

"I've lost the child," she sobbed.

The child was ahead of her on the snow, crying. Why was she looking for the child? He looked at her, astonished. Then he said: "I'll take the child; the little man's already too heavy for his mother. It's the father who must teach a child to walk in the forest."

"Victor, will we soon be home?"

"It's still far away, Virginie. The snow is soft; the sun rotted it and then today there was that March avalanche. The snow sticks to your feet like dough to the kneading tray. We've still a long way to go, Virginie."

She could no longer hide it from him.

"I want to stay here."

"I can't carry you, Virginie. But I can carry the child."

The man picked up the child.

"I'll give you the rifle and leave you here and walk to the monastery. But don't stay there: try and walk a little so you won't get chilblains. Fatigue is like sleep. You must wake up, Virginie. Move a little, take a few steps. You mustn't let yourself be caught by the cold. Walk. Follow my tracks. I'm going to go to the monastery and I'll put our child by the fire there and give him some gruel, then we'll come for you. It will be night, but don't be frightened; your eyes get used to the dark and they can see as if it was day. Don't be frightened, follow my tracks, walk slowly, but don't stop. The earth will be covered by night when we come back. Virginie, don't let go of your rifle: only fire at a wolf or a bear. Don't waste your bullets. It's a long way to our cabin, Virginie, but we'll sleep there tonight. Walk: running water doesn't turn to ice. Walk. I'll leave the cow with you. If you're too cold, huddle close to the cow, she's as warm as good fresh milk. If you don't see my tracks in the snow because the blizzard's erased them, let her lead you; she knows where I'll be. Walk, Virginie. A woman who can make a child can walk in the snow, even if it's higher than the treetops. The cow's up ahead, where I left her. I'm taking the child to the monks' warm fireside. And when he's lying by the fire I'll come back here."

He took a few steps with the child and they vanished like a cloud. She was alone now, surrounded by raging snow. She must walk. Why? Because her man had told her to walk. A woman must obey her man. She walked, but what she wanted to do was sleep: to sleep in a bed, to sleep pressed against the warm body of her man. How long had she walked with the child in her arms? How long had she walked, dragging the heavy rifle? Her man had told her to walk to escape the cold, but the cold was moving faster than she, and she could feel it in her bones. She called to her man. She stopped and waited for the reply. There was only the silence of the snow. Dry sounds like bones colliding in the wind. Weren't there skeletons hanging from the spruce trees? Hadn't skeletons accompanied her through the blizzard? She was travelling through the land of death, where she shouldn't have ventured. Skeletons swayed and tolled in the wind about her, but she mustn't fire. The man had told her to kill only wolves or bears. The man wasn't answering her, so he must be far away with the child. Perhaps they'd already reached the monastery. The snow was falling even thicker. The skeletons were still around her, hidden in the storm, rattling their bones. The rifle wasn't made for a woman: it was heavy. A man's rifle. If the skeletons hadn't been lying in wait for her she would have abandoned it in the snow. She had been walking for such a long time. Her body was cold. It must be night. Exhausted as she was, she hadn't stopped walking, pushing away the snow that was as heavy as stone. In her hand the rifle had become a heavy icicle. The snow was closing in around her. She had read a story like this in school: the snow was quicksand. Had it swallowed up her man and her child? Had she herself been swallowed up? She thought she was still alive, but wasn't this a dream? She was going to die. She felt so sleepy. Wasn't dying like falling asleep? Was she already asleep? And the snow, the storm, her man who had disappeared, and her child—weren't they only dreams? She was so tired. The ice around her was only a dream. She felt warm. She was as comfortable as her child in the monastery, before a fire, drinking milk. She wasn't hungry. Soon her man would come for her. She congratulated herself for having taken his advice. Leaning against the cow she fell asleep in the animal's warmth.

* * * * *

F irst, the monks had built a cabin from squared-off trunks, to house three of them, and a lean-to—the chapel. Sheltered, then, the three monks had started to build for the future: young men would come from all over America to this refuge to which God would call them, far from worldly temptations. And around the cabin and the chapel, they had started to erect the walls of the future monastery. Winter had come too soon, though. The men who had come to help them had gone back to their villages. The monks stayed on alone. The unfinished walls of the future monastery formed a palisade around the cabin. There the monks felt safe from wild animals and winds. That night, filled with warmth and prayers. They weren't worried about the wind, which was exceptionally violent for this time of year when spring was already approaching beyond the horizon. Bending over their Latin books, they celebrated God's goodness: His hand had guided them to this savage land where they would build a house for His children. The restless dogs were growling and lingering insistently in the chapel. The old monk kept going back to the same line on his page: in the end he'd forgotten what was said at the beginning. It was all because of the howling wolf. He had never heard a wolf with such a cry. The two young monks could hear it too, for they were applying themselves so ostentatiously to their prayer, they must be distracted by it. The wolf was howling as if struggling to utter human sounds. The old man was not alone in his concern, for his two colleagues looked up from their books, then looked questioningly at each other. The fire was purring in the hearth, then suddenly it grew restless as a gust of wind passed over the chimney. They listened to the night. The dogs were worried. The walls creaked, shaken by the wind, creaked like the boat that had brought the monks to this country. A wolf couldn't howl like a man. It was impossible for a man to be in the forest, during such a storm. The monks were the only human beings in the forest. The previous village was a good day's journey by sleigh. On the other side, there had always been only one cabin, Victor's, and Victor had gone to Quebec for his wife. A wolf howling human cries on a stormy night? It was the Devil prowling around the house of God. Only he knew the language of wolves and of men. The monks traced a cross on their breasts; the sign reminded them that the Son of God had come to earth and died so as to trample Satan. In the storm the Devil didn't take flight at this sign as he usually did. The dogs were barking. The monks listened: he was certainly inside the palisade and coming closer to their cabin. He was howling like a man calling for help. The Devil wouldn't have called for help. The door was rattling. It couldn't be the Devil; someone was crying outside. The dogs jumped against the door. The monks left the chapel. Someone was sobbing bitterly and trying to break down the door. The monks drew back the bolts: pushed by the wind, the door slammed. A man collapsed on the floor. The dogs leapt on him. The man wasn't walking erect like a man, but on all fours. Ice and snow were stuck to his clothes, as if to the fur of a beast. The old monk shouted an order to the dogs. They smelled the man and finally went back to the fire. It was a man and he was weeping. The monks grasped his arms and led him to the hearth, next to the dogs. One of the young monks threw some logs on the fire, while the other took a broom and began to brush the snow and ice from his clothes. The old man went into the chapel, drew a small key from his soutane, opened the padlock on the chest in which the mass wine was stored and took out a flask of Dutch gin that the good Lord had inspired him to keep there, like a precious drug. Was the man weeping? It seemed to the monks he was laughing. "At times of great sorrow, people sometimes laugh," said the old monk. "Some sorrows are too great to be expressed by tears; to give voice to all the pain it's sometimes necessary to laugh." The man was laughing. The monk held the flask of Dutch gin. Perhaps he's already drunk, drunk too much. But if he was drunk, how could he have found the monastery in this snow that was denser than the most tenacious fog? They recognized Victor, who had spent some months with them helping them build the monastery.

"Have you come back to us, Victor?"

"Are you bringing us fine weather, Victor?"

"Victor, you promised to come back with your wife and child. Did you bring them? Have them come in."

Suddenly Victor got to his feet. He was laughing in a way the monks would never have dreamed he could laugh. Was he drunk? The monk brought the flask of gin closer to him; he did not reach out his hand for it.

"In such weather, Victor, your stomach must be filled with frost."

He didn't even glance at the flask, but started taking off his wet clothes, and he laughed in a booming voice that filled the cabin. This man whom they'd known to be timid, who would blush if one of the workmen started telling a story he knew would have a spicy ending, took off all his clothes in front of the monks, then dropped onto a straw mattress as bare as the Baby Jesus in His crib. The old monk gestured to the young ones to cover him. Soon his body, shaken by tumultuous laughter, no longer moved. He wasn't laughing now, but snoring. The dogs came and lay by his pallet. Victor, his wife and his child were to form the first family in the parish that would spread out around the monastery. He had returned alone, coming out of the storm. He had entered the monastery behaving like a tracked man. This man who was laughing like a maniac wasn't the Victor the monks had known last summer, who applied himself to his work with an axe and a two-handed saw like a child bending over his first scribbler. Then, he never laughed. He wasn't sad but he thought that men, beasts and things are held in the hand of God, and that laughter made fun of the way that God held them. When he stopped working he would talk at length; he talked like a confident man. And when he talked you could believe that he already saw, where tangled spruce now stood, his land surrounded by farms, and the sawmill, the school, the chapel. That was the man whom the monks had known during the summer, who had appeared suddenly out of the storm, prostrate, laughing or crying, who had stripped and vanished into sleep as if he were drunk. And yet he had refused the drink they offered him. When they asked him about his wife and child, his torrential laughter had covered the monks' questions. The storm had turned the man into a wild beast. Calm now under the covers, he slept. The Devil had no doubt left his body and gone back into the storm. He was roaring in the wind. Victor had not come back alone. One of the monks started to shake him.

"Where did you leave your wife and child? Victor!

Answer! You didn't come by yourself! Victor! Where did you leave them?"

From the depths of his sleep he was snoring. The two young monks slipped coats over their soutanes, pulled on boots and fur hats, lit torches, tied knives to their belts and took up rifles. The dogs had got up and were scratching at the door: they realized that they were going to be harnessed to the sleigh. The old monk stayed behind to pray. He prayed for a long time. Victor was an exhausted man. Victor was snoring as if he was going to sleep for three days. The monk prayed, certain that some disaster had occurred. Victor wasn't supposed to come back by himself: he was supposed to bring with him his wife and child. And the snowstorm had cast him up alone, like a man left on the shore by a shipwreck. The monk prayed. Who, then, had offended God so much that He was dealing so harshly? The old monk didn't understand, and so he prayed. He thanked the good Lord for giving him the privilege of becoming a monk. Monks had the mission of listening to the voice of God when other men were busy with their work, or snoring. But he didn't understand God's message in this storm and so he prayed. He prayed for a long time. Several times he threw logs on the fire. He replaced the candles on the altar. Several times he fell asleep on his breviary, but he woke up right away: a feeling of guilt wrenched his soul, for the good servant must not sleep when he is charged with watching and with listening to the voice of God who speaks to men in storms. Victor was snoring. He no longer had a soul, he had been made mindless by the happiness of sleep. For didn't sleep mean to live only through one's body? A monk should live only through his soul. He struggled to keep his body from succumbing to sleep. His soul must be attentive. And he prayed. Little flames had already devoured the new candles. He must replace them again and, once again, feed some logs to the voracious fire. Outside, the snowstorm, too, seemed to want to sleep. Was it his imagination that made him hear what he wanted to hear? Dogs were barking. Far away. His soul no longer wanted to pray. Dogs were truly barking. His colleagues were returning. God had guided them through the night. Then God was still protecting His monks. The dogs were barking in the enclosure around the monastery. The old monk opened the door. It had stopped snowing. The wind was no longer blowing. But the air felt as sharp on his face as if it were January. His colleagues were bringing someone with them. Bending over the sleigh, they picked up a body wrapped in blankets. Had God struck someone down in the forest?

"Brothers, do you bring life or death?"

"Praise be to God: we bring life!"

"God blesses us!"

"She is alive. Praise be to God!"

The two monks brought Virginie into the cabin. They asked her questions. She did not hear them. She did not see them. Was she even aware that they had brought her here on a sleigh pulled by dogs? Its runners had struck an obstacle. The monks had stopped. It was an abandoned rifle. The dogs had found Virginie a few steps further, covered with snow. She seemed so lifeless that the monks had started to pray for the repose of her soul. The monks dared not touch this woman lying by the fire. They dared not take her ice-soaked clothing from her body. To avoid having their hands, the hands of consecrated men, come in contact with this woman's body, they threw blankets on the floor and wrapped her in them. Suddenly, words rose to her mouth, distorted by her lips that were sealed by the cold. Had the monks heard correctly? Had she not asked for her child? She had said: "My child?" She was calling for her child. Victor had come as announced, then, bringing wife and child. But where was the child? The old monk's gaze questioned his colleagues. Astonishment. They hadn't seen the child. "He's sleeping, your child, he's sleeping very peacefully," whispered the monk. The young woman sighed and continued to sleep before the fire. The monk didn't ask God's pardon for not having told the truth: he had not lied. If the child had been lost in the snowstorm, he was sleeping in the land of the angels now. It was a great catastrophe that God had sent to the forest to test this man and woman but, the old monk thought, what man can determine if God's acts are a curse or a blessing? With similar gestures the monks joined their hands, bowed their heads and prayed for a moment: the child who had died on the parish land would be their first angel, and he would transmit to God the prayers of those who dwelt on this corner of the earth. The two younger monks set out again with the dogs, who barked as if they were celebrating, to search for the little lost body. The old monk put more logs on the hearth, replaced the burnt-out candles on the altar and began his prayers again. The man and the woman would awaken (he almost said they'd be resurrected), and the old monk would need words that go to the heart. He must find inspired words, he must explain that which cannot be understood, he must make them agree to submit to God's will. The monk prayed for a long time. When his colleagues returned, he didn't hear the barking dogs: he had dozed off at his prie-Dieu. Victor sprang from his pallet, frightened.

"Wolves! Wolves! I've been expecting you! I can howl louder than you. Wolves! Don't come any closer! Go away! I'll strangle you!"

The dogs threw themselves at him, and he yelped louder than the animals. Then they recoiled. The good Lord had not directed the young monks to the child who was lost in the forest. Opening the door, they saw a naked man who gesticulated as he howled a wordless lament; he was howling like a wild beast, a wounded beast. The old monk had awakened: "God, why does the life of Your children sometimes resemble a nightmare? No, God, don't answer, I'm not worthy of understanding, but I am listening to Your voice." The blankets were stirring before the hearth where the fire was dying down. The young woman murmured,

"Is the child here?"

A man cried out:

"No!"

The young woman burst out of the covers and threw herself at Victor. The three monks, who didn't know the woman, decided to withdraw so that one of life's mysteries might come to pass. The man and woman were screaming like wild beasts that might bite each other. Was this their way of showing love? In the morning cold the monks shivered and prayed in the chapel. The dogs barked in response to the cries from the monastery. Then, all was calm. The monastery became silent again. The silence of God was restored to His kingdom. Suddenly Victor rushed into the chapel.

"I've lost him in the blizzard, I lost the child, but I know where I lost him, and God knows I haven't abandoned him, I haven't abandoned the child! I've lost him, but God will help me find him. I'll come and show him to you, he's the first child in the parish: God couldn't have taken him away from me! I'll find him, I'll find the child!"

Naked, in snow to his chest, he was already leaping about like a deer.

"We'll go with you," said the old monk. "My brothers and the dogs will help you."

The old monk came inside, helpless and timid in the presence of the woman who was not sleeping now, who was weeping.

"That man," she said, "has killed my child."

*   *   *   *   *

F or several weeks, the bearskin was stretched out like the sail of a motionless ship. The man walked up to it, stroked the fur, patted the front and back of the skin, then tightened the rope that attached it to the birch frame. One day, Virginie saw him cut the rope. The skin fell onto him, and she couldn't help thinking that the savage fur was quite appropriate for that man who had killed a child. He admitted to the monks that he had placed the child where he would be sheltered from wind and snow while the man rested. That morning when he was growling, naked, in the monastery, like an enraged bear, he admitted that the child had become heavy as a stone in his arms and that he had set it down under the branches, beside the sack of provisions. He had rested, then gone on his way again, forgetting the sack and the child. How could he have rested from the storm without holding the child against his chest, to pass on the warmth of his body? The branches didn't keep the wind from digging its cold claws into the little body. The man had slept, then set off again, alone, as if he had never bestowed life on a child, as if there had been nothing but snow under the branches, as if the ice of the cold little body had been like the ice on which he had struck his foot. He had set off again as if he weren't responsible for preserving the breath in the child's little body. He confessed it to the monks: he had forgotten the sack and the child. The snow had piled up, erasing the child. He kept on walking as if he were alone. A man has no right to forget that he has bestowed life. A man has no right to be concerned only with the great breath of the winds, no right to lose interest in the small breath of a child who is trying not to die. That man has bestowed death; he must be punished. His punishment must be harsher than death, if the good Lord is just. And the Lord is just. The author of life does not forgive a man who has bestowed death. The Lady of olden times, whose soul journeyed from generation to generation, through stories, to Virginie, will help her in the task of punishing that man. The sound of chains that she can hear far away, in an old memory, is music now and no longer frightens her. July has come. He will die in July, that man who threw her child into a snowstorm rather than carry him in his arms to the monastery fire. If the good Lord hadn't wanted her to bestow death on this man, He wouldn't have allowed July to come, or He wouldn't have allowed her to reach July, or He wouldn't have allowed deadly plants to grow. The good Lord will dispense justice: it is He who created poison. Virginie's hands will gather the plants, but in her hands there dwells the soul of the Lady whom the good Lord has permitted to roam the earth and appropriate her body. Everything that happens is due to God's will. He wants her to punish that man. Why did God want the child's death? She doesn't understand. God doesn't want a simple woman to understand the mysteries of life and death. Once she has bestowed death, the good Lord will abandon her and men will lead her to a dungeon cell, to damp straw; at every step her chains will ring out on the stones. After several years a great ship will come for her and carry her across the sea; there, someone will toss a cloak over her shoulders, someone will open his arms and she will begin a new life. It is possible, too, that men will tie a rope around her neck and hang her on the Place du Marché. She doesn't shudder in fright at the thought of a hemp rope tied around her neck, squeezing her, and of her body weighing heavily at the end of the rope. When the man bursts through the door, covered by the bearskin, she sees only the wild animal that tried to come in the window, that broke down the wall. He sets the bearskin down by the pallet where Virginie sleeps; he unrolls it, spreads it out, strokes the fur. Then he lights a candle, for it is already dark.

"Your feet won't ever be cold again, Virginie. I didn't like to see your little woman's feet on the log floor, with knots as prickly as thorns. Now you'll set your feet on this fine bearskin, and I know there are plenty of great ladies in the Upper Town of Quebec who don't have fur to set their feet on when they get up; but you, when you get up, your feet will step in softness like the Queen of England. Oh, Virginie! if the good Lord thinks of me, you won't always live in a cabin where bears try to break in; think of the house where you'd like to live and I'll build it for you, I'll build it so solid, it'll still be standing a hundred years from now. And you won't always live in the woods: I'm going to make fields for you, all around the house. The trees have already started to move back. You won't always be alone. Other cabins will be built around the monastery. The forest will move back around those cabins. The cabins will become fine painted houses, Virginie. We're going to build a road and we'll have horses and a cart. We'll be able to go to the next village. Every year, Virginie, we'll be able to go to the City of Quebec; you'll be able to see your parents. We'll show them our children. If you wanted, we could show them a new child on every visit. You mustn't think about our catastrophe. It's July now, and July's the time for life. If the good Lord has put us to a test the way He tests His faithful servants, it's because He wanted to be sure we were worthy of all the blessings He was going to rain down on us. Virginie, I talked about rain and it's starting to rain. This shower will be good for the earth. We'll have fine potatoes in September, if the good Lord protects us from the raccoons, and at the end of August we'll have fine corn. Last July there was nothing but trees, Virginie, nothing but trees and the forest. The good Lord loves us!"

The time has come for the bestowing of death. That man must be punished even unto his descendants. She walks along the outstretched bearskin. Fixing her gaze on the man's, a gaze as hard as if she would put out his eyes, without a word she starts to undress. The click of buttons, the swish of falling cotton and homespun. This woman's body, which he is seeing naked for the first time, stuns him as if lightning has struck his face. He can no longer breathe. His legs no longer support him. He falters, his arms stretched in front of him like a bear's paws, toward Virginie, who throws herself on the floor with him. They roll in the fur. An animal's raucous breathing. The man jostles her, embraces her, holds her, crushes her, does his best to break her bones. She endures it all. The child he will cause to be born in her belly will be shut away in the dungeon cell too. If she is hanged from the neck by a rope at the stake, the child in her belly will be hanged as well.

* * * * *

T hat man is talking. Virginie does not listen.

"Life's beginning again. I've seeded you, Virginie. You've become my land again. If the good Lord still loves us, your body will be fertile. We have land, Virginie, but since the good Lord's allowed us to start our life over, I'm going to walk in the woods and pick the finest piece of land I see, and add it to our land; then when my life is over I'll have land to give to that child."

Suddenly she hears:

"I'll be going pretty far, Virginie. Now don't worry. The good Lord makes the days long in July because He knows that a man who works on his land needs plenty of light. And if it's dark and I'm not back yet, don't worry, I'll sleep under the good Lord's stars. I'll leave you the rifle. I know you can use it as well as a man."

Soon the man's snoring covered his words. She cannot sleep beside that man. Nor could the Lady who had chains at her ankles sleep when the guards who had brought her along a deserted road, in an unknown direction, were snoring near her. She remembers those nights when it seemed that dawn would never return to light the earth. She remembers endless nights when she hoped for dawn as she might hope for cold water after an endless walk. She would like to go out at once, and walk toward the rim of the forest. But the night is dense. She would see nothing. Lying on her back, she examines the dark ceiling; she is waiting for the sparks of dawn that soon will burst through the logs, the moss and the birchbark. Then she will go out. But the night lingers on. Like a winter that won't accept the coming of spring. The Lady's story was Virginie's too: Virginie lived centuries ago and the Lady who lived in those olden times is alive today. Just as she waited for the dawn so many years ago, somewhere in the pitch-black night, so she waits today, here in this cabin. The dead child knew his future too. That's why he cried so hopelessly. In his little head, incapable of uttering words, he knew that man was going to give him to the storm. That man knows he is going to die. Otherwise, would he have told her that he wouldn't be back tonight, but would sleep under the stars? He knows he will be struck down to the ground, and his dull gaze will seek an answer in the silent sky. He will imitate the child in the snow, by the tree, crying to heaven that gave no reply. That man's eyes will resemble the eyes of the child that were dimmed because death was rising through his body. That man knows he is to die tomorrow. Tomorrow he will sleep under the stars, but it will be a silent sleep. She will go to a dungeon cell. The Lady will go to a dungeon cell. The ceiling is implacably dark. The forest is still drenched in night: she doesn't dare go out. The night makes strange everything that it touches: trees become emaciated phantoms; the earth beneath her feet is changed into sinister mud; the wind becomes sorrow and the sky itself is like an abyss in which she might fall. Suddenly a spot of light pierces the ceiling, too brilliant to be dawn. She must have dozed off. It is morning.

She rises. That man goes on sleeping, as if night still held sway. The wooden hinges creak. That man mustn't be awakened. She opens the door, as little as possible. She is naked. That man must not be awakened. She runs in the forest. Beneath her feet she feels neither pebbles nor twigs nor thorns. This morning the birds do not sing. She knows where she is going. Close to the forest, devil's bread grows. "Those mushrooms are deadly poison; you mustn't touch them; they're devil's bread." Near the woods which that man hasn't yet attacked grows enough bread for the devil to eat his fill for a long time. The good Lord wants her to dispense justice. And now the devil will help her. Can she touch these lethal plants without danger? Their caps are the color of glowing coals. Devil's bread resembles devil's fire. The mushrooms are covered with disgusting warts. The devil's skin must be like that. She must look a long time for the devil's bread. When at last she has found it, scattered around the outskirts of the forest like the remains of loaves multiplied not by God as in the Bible, but by the devil, she wants to know if it contains the deadly poison. She bends down and rubs it on the silver ring she has worn since her wedding day. The ring turns black. The good Lord, who has sown all about them animals and plants that they could eat, has also allowed the devil to distribute his poison food. She will dispense justice. Briskly, she kneels and pulls up some mushrooms. She already has an armful which she holds against her breasts. It feels cool. She is bearing death. How soft it feels, the death that she carries on her breast! She tries to run, for she must return before that man awakens. Grass wet with dew tangles around her legs, holding her back. It feels as cold as snow. She hurries. Why is she thinking of snow when the sun's fire is burning the sky? She pushes the door. Creaking. The man shakes himself and turns on the mattress. If he catches sight of her with the devil's bread, he won't want to eat what her hands have touched. She

113

tosses the devil's bread in a pot and covers it. He opens his
eyes. The light that comes in the door is hurting them. He
shuts them for a moment, then gets up. Without speaking, he
arranges dry wood in the stove, shreds some birchbark, lights
it and, when the fire has caught, he takes the buckets to the
stream. He is going to draw the water that will kill him. He
returns, singing, wet: he has rolled in the cool water. She
pours some water into the kettle, then into the pot with the
mushrooms, and a little bowl where she has put buckwheat
flour.

"What a sleep, Virginie! I haven't slept like that for ages.
Some nights I come home so worn out I can feel my body
behind me at the end of a rope, like a horse that refuses to
move: even on nights like that I don't sleep like I slept last
night. Virginie, I slept like the dead. I tell you, a man who
slept the way I did can't still be alive."

Virginie dresses briskly. That man shouldn't have seen
her naked. In the pot the mushrooms are boiling. Gray scum
is raising the lid. She spreads buckwheat batter on the metal
plate of the stove.

"I'll make you some chicory coffee too, for your journey.
I'll pour it in a bottle. Once you've travelled a good distance,
find a tree with thick roots, and sit and rest your back against
the tree and drink the coffee. Then you won't feel tired any
more."

Did he notice that she was speaking? He eats his buckwheat pancake with syrup from the maples he tapped that
spring. Virginie's hand doesn't tremble as she pours the
poisoned water into the bottle. She adds two handfuls of
chicory, then pushes in the wooden stopper. She places the
bottle in the heavy canvas sack along with a blanket, the axe,
the wire for making snares. That man is so happy he feels like
dancing.

"Our life had stopped as if we were dead, Virginie, just the length of one tiny death, but we've come back to life! God is so good to us, Virginie!"

He picks up the sack, throws it over his shoulder and, like a man who is thinking of dancing, who hears mad music, he goes gaily into the forest. The neck of the poisoned bottle gleams in the sun, for it protrudes from the sack.

* * * * *

Now, she waits. Perhaps that man will come back tonight. He will have walked, walked, always thinking of his land, larger now, and of the children who will help him to clear it of trees, to plough, to sow, children whose cries will mingle with those of the birds. He will have walked from tree to tree, adding them up like a rich man counting his pieces of gold; in his mind he will have felled these trees, chained them together and hauled them to the forest track, he will have transported them to the sawmill and sold them as boards and beams, and he will have pulled up the stumps and ploughed the soil in his dream, as if it were reality. Crammed with these thoughts, he will have forgotten to eat, he will not have brought the bottle of poison to his lips. He will return. She will see him suddenly burst out of the forest like a rutting moose, quivering, his great nostrils filled with the female's odor, taking great strides, for he has conquered new land and is set to seize his wife who cannot resist him, for he has decided that life has begun again. She waits. She sits on the pile of wood that is heaped up in anticipation of winter. Flies are desperately going at her face and neck, but she is indifferent to them. That man is going to come out of the woods. She waits for him. She has not succeeded in dispensing justice. She has not succeeded in killing that man, who thinks he can replace a child who was killed on a stormy night with a child who was made in July. He approaches. He will burst in, lowing like an animal who sees the female. She has not killed him. She is not the Lady who had chains at her ankles. In the solitude of this forest she has told herself a tale. He is not dead. She will never go to a dungeon cell. That man will emerge from the forest; like a great moose, he will shake his antlers, bellowing that he is alive, that he wants to mount the female. She will never be in chains. He is alive. She will never go to a dungeon cell, onto rotting straw. Her man will return. He will never know that there was poison in his sack. She has listened too hard to the voices of the wind in the spruce trees, she has listened too hard to stories from the past. That man is alive. She is not a Lady who knows how to prepare poison, she will never be chained up in a dungeon cell, she will never be deported on a many-masted ship. She is only an innocent young woman who has left her parents in the city of Quebec and followed into the forest a man with whom she once danced to the music of magical violins. She is only a young woman who sits on a log, waiting for her man who has gone into the woods. She should put the potatoes on to boil for his meal. She does not know how to kill. The leaves will part and he will appear. She didn't want to kill. If she had, she would have taken the rifle and shot him the way she shot the bear. She is only an innocent young woman who never wanted to kill. She is a young woman alone in the forest, and the wind was bringing her echoes of time past. Her soul has become so sad. Evening veils the trees. Her eyes no longer see to the rim of the woods.

She goes back inside the cabin. She does not light a candle or the fire in the stove. He will return tomorrow. The territory he wants to explore is vast. Luckily he took a blanket. Tomorrow she will go and bury the rest of the devil's bread that has formed a paste in the bottom of the pot. She waits for dawn, sitting on her pallet, her feet in the black bear's fur. Just now, that man must be lying on the ground, his eyes gazing at the stars. Has he drunk the poison? She thinks she'll never get to sleep tonight. However, she is already asleep. And not realizing that she is asleep, she is struggling, one step at a time, through deep snow. Each step is difficult: the snow pushes her backwards, her feet are as heavy as tree-stumps, with roots that clutch at the ground, and the snow lashes her face. In the driving snow she can no longer see the trees, but she's not concerned: her child is in the arms of his father, who protects him as if he were his own heart. There is so much snow. Where is the passage through the trees? Where are the trees? Where is she? Her body is limp, as if she were asleep. Beyond her, the man holds the child in his arms and he will carry him through the storm. The snow lashes her face and she must keep her eyes shut. Often, men and horses fall asleep during blizzards and die. She must not fall asleep. She must keep her eyes open. She lifts her head. There is no snow. It is not night. The light pierces sparkling holes in the roof. The man is somewhere in the forest. The child is no longer in the forest. The man, perhaps, is alive. The child is dead. Now she will wait until evening. That man told her he would sleep one night in the forest. At dusk she will see him appear. If he didn't drink the poison yesterday, he will be thirsty when he wakes up this morning under his blanket; he will light a fire and boil up his chicory coffee; when he brings it to his lips it won't taste as it usually does, but he'll be thirsty and he'll think about how far he must walk to reach his cabin. He will drink the poison to the last drop. And so she won't see him return this evening. She will wait. She waits for evening to come. All day long it seems to Virginie that the sun is clinging to the same point in the sky, not moving toward where it will set. She has not eaten. She watches the forest intently, beneath the unmoving sun. Why does she keep her gaze fixed on the rim of the woods? If he is alive he'll return. If he has drunk the poison, it's pointless to wait: the wild animals have probably already attacked his remains. What is it that keeps her gaze fixed on the trees throughout this long day? Does she hope he will return? Does she hope that she hasn't killed him? Death cannot be corrected like a mistake in a schoolchild's scribbler. Death endures. It cannot be erased and so it must be punished. On the wall of distant trees she tries to decipher the signs of her fate. If that man does not appear she will die; and if her man lives, she will live. Only the forest seems alive. She is dazed from watching a sun that does not move. Is she still alive? Her man is dead, she has killed. In the great light-filled sky, nothing moves. Time is motionless. The forest is empty now of the cries of birds. Their flights have been interrupted. Even the wind has touched down on the branches without disturbing them. Already there are fastened about her ankles the endless links of an invisible chain which attach her to an unknown point in the forest where a man has been struck down. She waits. That man is dead and his life will be stopped around her forever, like an implacable wall. Henceforth the days will be long, the nights unending. Will there be a difference, in her dungeon cell, between the days and the nights? They will clutch at her like tenacious memories. Endlessly she will begin the same day; endlessly she will begin the same night, the same weaving always, that will always come undone. She will have but one memory, in which the brutal snow of a winter's night will mingle with the gentle silence of a summer's night when the body of a child abandoned in the snow will be confused with that of a man who has fallen among the spruce needles. Perhaps she won't even have any memories if she's tied by the neck to the gallows. At times shadows play on the branches, then seem to part, pushed by the body of a man. He cannot emerge from the forest, for he is lying somewhere on the ground, like a dead branch. Tomorrow, in the morning, she will go to the monastery. She will confess to the monk. She has not committed a sin, but she will go and kneel before the monk. He knows that the man has abandoned a child behind him, in the storm that blazed like a white fire. Can a monk erase the sin of having killed a man? There is a death and that death is just. That man is not to return. Why, then, does she watch the outskirts of the forest so intently? Would she have him return? She must not hope. How will she dress to go to the monastery? It has been so long since she has left the cabin. Has she so many dresses that she must hesitate before she chooses one? She will go to the monk dressed as she is, in this grey skirt that is frayed from trailing on the ground. She will not use coquetry to disguise her sin. She has not sinned. The child is powerless against its father. The child could never seek revenge. The mother has dealt the blow. She was no longer the woman who had loved that man. Men and women are submissive to laws that the blood obeys. Killing that man, she was obedient. How could obedience be a sin? When she goes to confess to the old monk, she will kneel at his feet and confess in a low voice that she poisoned the man. The monk will ask if she regrets her sin. One does not regret things that must be done. She will answer that she regrets it. But her soul will know that if that man miraculously came back to life she would prepare another poison. She will lie just as she killed: she must. The monk will forgive her and pray in Latin. After her confession she will be silent, a woman already condemned. Night, which has long since fallen, envelops her as if she were blind. Groping her way, she advances toward the cabin. She has forgotten to eat. Beyond her, that man has not eaten either. She will go to the monastery and confess her crime as soon as it's light again. Tonight it seems that morning is once again refusing to be born. For several hours she has been stretched out on the pallet. Her man, too, is stretched out in the night. Have wild beasts torn his body to pieces? Virginie's body, too, is made of flesh and animals could be attracted to it. Did she bolt the door? Trembling, she rises. Henceforth every day, every night will be infinitely long. She sets the door ajar to see if dawn is drawing near. The spruce trees blend with the night. All is night. She has killed. She shuts the door. Her soul has sinned. Does the good Lord no longer want to light the earth where she lives with her sin? If the night has no end she will leave, groping, she will find her way in the great dark disorder of the forest, she will wash her soul in the monk's orisons. She sits, fully dressed, on her pallet. She waits. Suddenly the light pounces on her brutally. She is dazzled. She has slept. Perhaps for a long time. It seems late in the day. She rushes out of the cabin. She will go to the monk. The day is filled with generous light. The spruce trees sparkle. She has been waiting so long for this moment when she will go to the monastery, where the old monk will weep as he listens to her. And what if that man returned? If he weren't dead? If he has escaped the poison? That man who always thinks of tomorrow has gone to explore the neighboring land with a view to enlarging his estate, but as he walked he must have realized that his land was very small and the forest very big. He wants to possess the whole forest. He must have walked with that idea in mind, like music, he must have walked the way he danced; he will have counted neither days nor nights, and he will turn up one evening, soon, perhaps tonight. He is not dead; you don't punish a man who was struck by disaster one night in a storm. If the raging winds take away his child, that man suffers as much as if his own heart were torn out. If that man is as strong as if he had two hearts, he must not be

punished just because he didn't let the catastrophe over-
whelm him. She knows now what it means to grow old: to be
alone and abandoned and lost and helpless. But he will be
back soon, for before he went, he left his seed in her belly.
Why go and seek help at the monastery? He will appear,
bearded and starving and happy: he will push aside the
spruce boughs, and at the end of the cleared area he'll catch
sight of his cabin and wife, and he'll shout:

"Virginie!"

She waits. A woman must wait for the man. She knows
she will dance with that man again. She will dance until she is
numb. When he comes back she will throw herself in his arms,
they will whirl and dance and she'll invent the music with her
mouth. They haven't danced for so long. That man has
worked so hard. And she, a transplanted little city flower, has
found living hard; the forest is filled with souls returned from
time past and their voices sadden a young woman's thoughts.
she is not sad now. She is waiting. She stands in the sun, her
gaze turned toward the forest. He will return. She feels a little
living spark in her belly. She forgets the great black night of
the storm. The man will return. And then she will wait for the
child.

*　*　*　*　*

T he nights are longer and longer. She has gone several nights without sleeping, but now she hurls herself into sleep as if she were falling from a cliff without ever touching bottom. She sleeps until she is weary. She sleeps in the daytime as well; the light doesn't bother her. The light is not so different from the night. Sometimes she can make things out clearly in the night and often when she looks at the forest in the daytime, she thinks she is blind. He will not return. She will not see him emerge from the forest and exclaim:

"I'm not dead, Virginie, I'm alive!"

She has bent down to drink from the spring and she has seen her face, looking worn as if she were several years older. The water, usually so delectable, tastes like water left standing in a bucket. It wasn't she who poured poison into the chicory coffee. Someone was haunting the night and the forest, someone was living in the dried bodies of the trees, someone was singing in the plaintive winds, someone knew the language of the tall spruce trees. That Lady from distant lands and time past has poisoned the man. The Lady has seeped into Virginie as a story seeps into your memory, and possessed her. She had to obey. It was she who had chains at her ankles. Her life is a dungeon cell. She will never be able to forget that she poured poison into that man's coffee. That act was as real as his death. The devil doesn't want her to regret her crime. The devil doesn't want her to go and confess her sin to the monk who is building a refuge in the forest for those who pray to God. In the dense solitude of the forest, it's the devil who has awakened the story of the Lady that was told on certain windy winter nights in her childhood; it's the devil who was demanding justice for the dead child; it's the devil who dwells in the forest. Virginie can still flee. Her chains are not so strong they won't be broken by a prayer to God. She can flee. She runs. She is going to the monastery; she runs toward the house of God, lifting her skirt on her legs. She doesn't feel her chains. The spruce trees are running with her. Behind her, the devil grows breathless. She shouts to the sky and the forest: "I have killed!", and her confession echoes from mountain to mountain, and the birds, alarmed, take flight. She cannot lose herself in the branchy chaos of spruce trees; she runs toward the monastery. She has killed and now she will seek the old monk's pardon. Her crime is like a brand in her heart. Her feet are light. Nothing binds them now. She runs as if she has gone to the monastery a hundred times. She distinctly hears the sounds of saws and hammers. She hears birds calling from tree to tree. She hears the hushed and fleeting sounds of squirrels. She hears the pounding of her heart. She has started to live again. The monastery is bigger. The walls are longer. There are new roofs. Men bustle about, holding hammers or saws. Some wear a soutane. One night, during a storm, she entered this monastery. She has not been back. She asks for the old monk. He comes. She kneels. Everything goes very quickly. Everything will go very quickly now.

"Father, I have killed. A man. My man."

The old monk falters. He doesn't want to believe what he has heard. His face has turned pale.

"Come into the shade, my child; this sun is too harsh for an old man, and probably for a young woman's pale brow too."

"Forgive me Father, for I have sinned. I killed a man. I prepared the poison. I waited for the poison to burn him, then I came to confess."

She is relieved, liberated. She thinks of the vegetables she hasn't watered for several days; they must be thirsty.

"My daughter, you are admitting to a very grave sin."

The old monk has knelt down before her; he has shut his eyes, to pray or to avoid seeing her.

"I've killed my husband."

The old monk cannot remain on his knees; he struggles to his feet.

"That's a crime, my child: the good Lord gave you the gift of life; in His wisdom He created your body to bear life, and you have brought forth death."

"Before my husband's death, Father, I asked him to deposit the seed of life in my womb."

"My daughter, your child will be hanged in your womb when you are hanged at the end of a rope."

The ceremony is very long. The old monk doesn't stop talking; the vegetables will die of thirst. If she could go and water them now she would save them, despite the blazing sun and the dry ground.

"My child, have you really committed the sin you've confessed?"

In September the corn will be golden and the potatoes ripe. In the autumn the child will start to move in her belly. She will cord plenty of dry wood for the winter.

"You'll be hanged at the gallows, my child. And if you don't show sincere contrition for your dreadful sin you'll be damned. Do you sincerely regret your sin?"

"Father, I'm prepared to regret my sin from the bottom of my soul, if my regret would bring my husband back to life. But if my regret doesn't bring him back to life, it's pointless."

The old monk cannot speak. He whispers:

"If you have no regret, my child, you'll be damned and your lost soul will be condemned to wander in suffering for all eternity. I am not permitted to bless you, my child, if you feel no regret. Your soul will wander among all the sorrows that wander on this poor earth."

The old monk's voice abruptly becomes powerful.

"Take this damned soul to the gallows!"

Big man's hands swoop down on her. Everything will go quickly now.

* * * * *

S he falls, a wingless bird. Everything is going too quickly. She is surrounded by men who insult her in silence, who push her and jostle her. Some carry a rifle, others an axe. Is it to protect them from wild animals? Rather, it is she whom they fear; she can see in their eyes that these men who fear nothing are afraid of a woman who has killed a man. The group stops at the farm in the next village where she and that man had stopped before the catastrophe. She recognizes the house. The farmer comes out. His wife follows him. Then the children. She recognizes them. She remembers so well. They don't let themselves look at her. The woman pushes the children inside. The man hitches his horse to the cart. The woman doesn't want Virginie to get in their cart. "That carriage wasn't made for carting the devil!" The men climb into the cart. Virginie will follow behind. The cart clatters heavily through the pebbly mud. Once they are out of sight of the farmer's wife the men jump out of the cart and push Virginie in. The farmer runs away. "I don't want to sit next to a poisoning witch." She sits and pulls her skirt over her legs. The men look at her with violent hunger in their eyes. The farmer grabs his horse by the bridle: "Just in case the devil wants to make off with my horse, I'm keeping a grip on his mouth."

"The time we spent with that witch is time taken from the Lord's house. We ought to tie her to a tree and leave her for the bears!"

"Maybe bears are smarter than men; they'd keep their distance."

"May the good Lord help us to show this poor sinner Christian charity," said one of the young monks, who had lifted their soutanes above their knees so they wouldn't drag in the mud.

"Let us pray," said the other young monk, "that God's punishment won't strike His faithful servants who are taking the sinner to the gallows."

"We should hang her right away instead of praying, the way Christians hang murderesses; the judge can do his judging later."

"In the good old days they used to burn witches; I wonder why nowadays they treat these ladies to a brand-new rope. You even have to wear white gloves to make the knot."

Is she listening or not? She hears the men all around her, armed with forks, with rifles and sticks; they moan, they threaten, they blaspheme, they pray and they curse, but she's not afraid. She hears, but she feels as if she isn't there, amid these vociferating men. Rather, she is listening to the hubs purring against the axles. These men's voices are so far away, as in another time. A time she has already left. But the big iron-rimmed wheels are turning, sinking into the mud, rolling in the water of a river, striking pebbles, becoming mute in grass or moss, then suddenly rumbling on tufa. The wheels turn slowly; she could count the spokes, one by one. And yet, everything is going too fast. The wheel turns and she gazes at it, fascinated; each rotation removes her from the man who collapsed in the forest, the piece of land stripped of its spruce trees, the log cabin, the monastery. Even the men who surround her, their voices like barking dogs, seem far away. Everything is going too fast. Night is already advancing. She sees it coming over the trees. They have already passed through two villages. The churches resemble one another, with their steeples piercing the sky (and the cross she no longer dares to look at); the little houses stuck along the road resemble one another too; people run out to get a look at her; from village to village, the insults are the same. The wheel turns. Her body can no longer tolerate being bruised by the shaking. Her flesh burns on her bones. She would like to get up and get out of the cart: with each turn of the wheel she feels she is being lashed by a whip. She rises. The men order her to lie down, like a dog. These man are torturing her before they hang her. The jolts burn her body like fire. She can bear it no longer. She moans like a suffering beast.

"Let us pray, brothers! Pray that the witch's curses aren't visited on us or on our lands!"

Night has fallen. She can no longer see the wheel turn. Around her she sees nothing at all. The men form dark stains in the night for they are blacker than it. When will they take her down? Time has stopped. The wait for that man's return was so long, so long. Then, everything was violently set ablaze. Now everything is peaceful again: the fire of time is damped down. The cart is no longer moving. Laboriously, struggling painfully, she gets to her feet. There is a lighted window nearby.

"Get down!" roars a voice.

She is jostled toward the lighted window. Someone drags her into a house that smells of children's urine. There are several gathered around the table. Some are looking. Others are crying. Someone pulls her over to a trap-door in the floor. Someone pushes her onto the ladder. She touches the floor right away. The ladder is short. Someone throws her gunny-sacks that still smell of oats. The trap-door closes over her head. She understands that she will sleep there, in the cellar, wrapped in gunnysacks.

"There's cabbage soup for the men, but it won't be said that the cabbage the good Lord grew on our land went to feed a witch."

"Let her die the way she let her man die!"

"The next soup she puts in her belly will be prison broth."

"Let us pray. We'll ask God not to let that woman's sin seep into the wood of this house."

She hears them talking. Above her, the floor cracks and bends under the weight of their knees. She hears the murmured prayer. Then they rise. By groping, she has found the gunnysacks. She spreads them around her and sits down. Next to the sacks the earth is damp and cold. The night is pitch-black, darker than any she has known in the forest. No thread of light falls from the floor. Above her, feet are walking, everywhere, endlessly. She pulls spiderwebs from her face. She is in a dungeon cell, like the Lady who had chains at her ankles. Those men would have tied her up with the chains the horses used to pull felled trees, if they weren't afraid she'd cast a spell on them. The old monk didn't forgive her. The men won't forgive her. They will eat and sleep, then take her to the gallows. She had to kill that man. But why did she spend interminable days facing the rim of the forest, waiting for him to return? Was she hoping that she hadn't poisoned him? Did she hope that unrepentant man would triumph over poison? In her black soul she knows with certainty that she was waiting for the man's return only so she'd be sure of his death. She knows with somber certainty that if the man had returned, the male would have rushed at the female whom he hadn't smelled for several days. She would have let him approach and then, craftily, she would have fled into the cabin, uttering little cries. The man would have bellowed, unable to contain his pleasure at knowing the female could not escape him now; and that male without a past, that bearded animal perfumed with the odors of resin and sweat, seeing that the female was a prisoner in the cabin, would have rushed at her, bellowing. In the doorway, a shot would have ripped his head from his neck. In a great flash of blood, death would have struck him down. She would have felt no remorse. No sorrow. They are eating; she can smell through the floor, stronger than the musty odors of earth and night enclosed in this cellar, the aroma of cabbage in the soup that they lap from their bowls. Then, when their bellies are full, wanting to prove they aren't afraid of her, several will come and seize her. She doesn't fear them. She doesn't fear the night into which they have cast her. Those men think they're holding a young woman who stopped loving her man because the forest was less fun than the city, and that in order to return to the city of Quebec, she killed that man whom she detested as much as she hated the forest. A soul that roamed the great night winds now occupies her body; it has settled in there like the fire in the hearth, like the past in memory. Virginie no longer feels regret, she is not afraid, and she knows things that it takes hundreds of years to learn. She will live in a dungeon cell and her chains will drag behind her for a long time. One day she, too, will wander, in stories of time past that will be told from generation to generation, to which children will listen, hypnotized. One night one of those children will suffer a great misfortune. And then, in the wind, she will remember from her childhood the story of a Lady who had chains at her ankles because she poisoned her husband in the forest. Only the suffering child will truly understand Virginie's story. She will know why Virginie felt neither regret nor remorse. Today, in her cellar, Virginie knows that the Lady was convicted because she poisoned her man. Virginie remembers that death better than her own man's, in the forest. She sees once more the ship in the harbor. Will it take her away too? What magic will transform the gibbet into the mast of a ship with a great sail attached to it? A miracle from God? She shudders as the word crosses her mind. Henceforth her companion is the devil. It is through him that she knows neither fear nor remorse. The men must have finished eating.

They laugh now as if words are tickling their throats. She knows they've drunk alcohol. She hears: "Let us pray!"

"Let us pray," says one of the monks, "that drunkenness won't lead us to sin."

The men are going to come down. She is not alone in the gloom. The devil who helped her to prepare the poison won't abandon her. She will be strong against these men. The cry of a child, frightened as if an animal has bitten him: the child howls his sobs along with his words. Finally she understands. The child cannot sleep in his bed. The witch, he says, is showing her purple face at the window, and her mouth which looks like a dog's; even though she's been shut up in the cellar because she's a witch, she can go where she wants to. The child is choking with sobs, saying that he felt the witch's long cold hands on his legs, and the claws on her fingers. The child is terror-stricken. Between sobs, he howls words of dread: the witch is going to set fire to the house. Voices of other children weep with as much anguish as the first; they are as frightened as the first. They too have seen the green or purple face at their window; the witch's long icy hand has glided along their legs. All the children cry together, with the same fear. Their cries are as loud as if they were coming from children lost in a black forest. How could the children not be frightened, when these men tremble as they approach her? A voice more powerful than the children's:

"Husband, you will throw that witch out before she does too much harm! Husband, decide: do you want to sleep with the witch or your wife?"

The woman's sobs cover the children's. And her cries become so strident that the children's sobs are stilled.

"Why did you bring that murderess here? She has killed: why didn't you hang her from a spruce tree? Why didn't you smash her filthy brains with rocks like they did in the good old days of Jesus Christ?"

They open the trapdoor. Everything will go quickly

now. Her eyes had grown accustomed to the dark. They cannot bear the light. She is already outside. Because of the light she could see in the kitchen, now her eyes don't tolerate the night. They push her into the cart. Everything will go too quickly. The men have drunk. She's not afraid. They sing those songs that men bray when they've drunk. The cart starts moving. A torch lights the road ahead. Not one star pierces the sky. Why don't these men let her walk behind the cart? Are they afraid of losing her? Do they think they're too drunk to keep watch over her? Her body can no longer bear the jolting of the cart over the bumpy road. If she'd been whipped by the men she would have felt the same fire in her back. Everything will go much too quickly. The men, who were laughing as if they had vomited while they told their stories, aren't laughing now; nor are they singing. They walk in silence. She hears their footsteps crushing grass or nudging pebbles. They walk as if they were sleeping. She doesn't want to run away. She wants only to sleep. It's been so long since she has been able to sleep. She regrets nothing. She hopes for nothing. She can sleep. Sleeping is like dying. She is used to the brutal clattering of the cart. Her body no longer feels pain from the bumps. She feels as if she is in a rocking chair. Rocking. She doesn't really know the Lady who holds her on her knees, but she enjoys the warmth of her body, she enjoys the way the chair moves on its rockers. She has fallen asleep. The sound of chains in the distance is only the gentle sound of the Lady's jewels. She is a little girl who had a nightmare and now sits on the knees of the Lady, who reassures her. She sleeps, she is no longer afraid. The night is mild. Suddenly, light hurts her eyes again. It is day. She is blinded. Then her gaze is cleared of the dark dust of night and she can distinguish men around the cart, painted houses, distant fields. Isn't that the river over there, in the background, like a long prairie sown with blue oats? And on the other shore, the city of Quebec? Among these houses squeezed together is her parents' house. She does not wish to see it again. She is not her parents' daughter, or she would never have killed a man. Her parents' daughter had a child in her arms when she left their house and in the cart Virginie's arms are empty. Before her, somewhere, are the dungeon cell and the gallows. Ah! if everything could go faster . . . The cart wheels seem stuck in thick mud. She is stuck in time that does not pass. And yet, the cart is advancing. And yet, the men are walking. And yet, the horse is pulling between the shafts. They have come to the ferry that crosses the river. The other carriages move aside. People insult her. No one wants to get on the ferry that is taking the witch across. She crosses alone, in the cart, surrounded by the men who have accompanied her since the monastery.

"Let us pray," says one of the monks, "that the ferry doesn't sink under the Lord's curse.

"That witch could drown us all."

"Let us pray."

The men unfasten chains that hang from the cart and wind them around her body. That way she can't run away or jump in the water. The ferry leaves the shore. Those who didn't want to cross with her hope she'll founder in the river. Those who are with her insult those on the shore.

"If she goes down, we drown with her. We haven't killed anybody; we're just as good Christians as you. And we don't wish you bad luck."

The ferry comes ashore at Quebec. How do people know that she has killed? There are people waiting on the wharf. They insult her. They curse her. The men who surround the cart must shout threats, raise their fists, wave their rifles and sticks to make their way among the bystanders who swear, insult and threaten. She is not afraid. She knows these cobblestone streets. She knows these houses. She doesn't want to enter them. She will never enter them. Nor does she feel like walking on these streets. She knows these stones, these windows, these doors. She knows these sidewalks. But she doesn't remember herself as a child or a young girl living in this place. She remembers only the forest, she can see herself only at the log cabin. Around her the city turns like a great wheel. She has killed a man. On all sides people insult her. She is not afraid. Soon she will be in a safe place. The cart and the men who surround it go past her parents' house. She does not look. The woman who has killed a man doesn't want to see the child who once lived there. Ah! if only things could go more quickly. Teams of horses, laden carriages move aside before her, but it seems to her that her cart has stopped moving. Insults rain down on her. People have thrown stones. The cart climbs up toward the Upper Town. The great ladies of Quebec live in the Upper Town. She smiles. She hasn't smiled for so long. She has killed a man and she is smiling. She is so tired. She was so far away, in the forest. There were nights when she would have liked so much to be not in that cabin, where the north wind blew right through the walls, but in her parents' house filled with the warm aroma of beef roasted with potatoes and carrots and onions. The cart has stopped. With almost affectionate gestures, men help her stand and get down. She is so tired. So many nightmares have gone through her head. She was so frightened. Her thoughts have always been stormy. They have entered her soul, brought there by demented winds. She no longer knows what she has dreamed. She never asked to return to her father's house, not even when she was trembling with cold in the cabin, or with the fear that brought on the great silence filled with mute voices. She was supposed to stay with that man. She has killed him. Virginie has brought about his death. Is it less than love? On that man's face as he lay in the forest, there must have been a smile: the smile of a man who has got what he deserved. An imposing stone house, a castle. She knows what it is. She mounts the stairs. The men who came with her do not abandon her. Men in uniform descend the stairs. They do not insult her. They lead her to an open door. Behind a table piled with papers, a man in uniform awaits her.

"This Lady," says one of the monks, "has killed her husband. She has confessed, but she has shown no sincere regret. She has presented herself to the justice of God, but now she submits to the justice of men."

She is not afraid. She knows what will happen. It seems to her that she has already lived this moment. She smiles. The officer behind the table has dipped his pen in the inkwell.

"Family name. Christian name. Occupation. Age."

*　*　*　*　*

The man dressed in black is cleaning his spectacles with a big white handkerchief. He rubs each lens meticulously. He folds his big handkerchief and puts it in his pocket. Then he places his spectacles on his nose and solemnly hooks them behind his ears. He looks at her for the first time. As if she hadn't been before him for a long time, between his guards. He peers at her as if she were tiny, as if it were hard for him to see her. He examines her. Is he looking for some mark of her crime? In the end, he finds nothing. He sniffs. Then he rummages through a pile of dossiers, selects a sheet of paper, starts to read. "No, that's not what I'm looking for." He rummages again, starts reading to himself, murmuring: "Yes, that's the one . . ."

" 'I, the undersigned, Virginie . . .' Is that you, Virginie?"

"Yes, it's my baptismal name."

"I'm not asking if it's your name, I'm asking if it's you . . . It's you who the Court will judge. Not your name."

"It's me, Monsieur."

"I'm not Monsieur, I'm a judge. Say: Your Honor the Judge."

"It's me, Your Honor the Judge."

The irritating voice goes on:

" '... declare under oath sworn on the Holy Gospels, this nineteenth day of July in the year 1862, in the reign of her Most Gracious Majesty Queen Victoria, that I have committed murder with regard to my husband, Victor...' Your man's name was Victor? etc. etc... 'using for the crime a poison made of poisonous mushrooms known as devil's bread, that I cooked and poured into his chicory coffee. Under the same oath I declare that I committed the crime in full knowledge and in cold blood, and I recognize that the motive for my act was revenge, because that man had caused the death of my child. Recognizing my complete responsibility, and with sorrow but no remorse, I sign this confession in full freedom, placing myself in the hands of the justice of God, of Her Majesty the Queen and of men.' And it's signed... etc. etc. Hmmm... So, Virginie... Madame... So, Madame, you murdered your husband. Do you have evidence?"

"He's dead, Your Honor."

"Did you see the corpse?"

"He died in the woods, Your Honor, and the bears must've eaten him, Your Honor."

"And you think we can tie a knot around your neck and hang you from the gallows and open the little door under your feet without having evidence that you deserve it?"

"When a woman kills her man, Your Honor, she knows if she's killed him."

"What I know is that if a woman kills her man, she sheds tears. For me, that would be evidence. But your eyes are dry. Now let me talk to you about your man. He was walking in the forest, thinking of the child who's to be born next winter. He was dreaming about enlarging his land, to make a bigger legacy for his descendants. Suddenly he stops for a drink. He sits down. He takes the cork from the bottle that his wife filled with coffee. The aroma it gives off makes him think of his wife. That man's heart is too small for his love. Suddenly, after he takes a big gulp, his belly is filled with infernal fiery serpents. Those fiery serpents gradually crawl through his body. They enter his intestines, they bite everywhere. The man can't breathe, he's choking, he turns black as if he's been burned by fire. He can't even shout. He is deep in the woods, far from the cabin where he's left the woman he loves. He is too far away. The woman he loves cannot hear him. The poisoned man, burned by the poison, is already dead, but he still writhes in pain; even though he is dead, he is suffering, and his sweat is scalding. He is in pain and cannot call out to the only person in the world who might have helped him. The poison has made his throat swell. His face is as black as brushwood. He died not knowing that it was the woman he loved who made him drink the fatal poison. When I tell you now about that man who couldn't call on you to rescue him, do you think that you'd have gone if you had heard him?"

"Your Honor, if I'd heard him calling me to rescue him I'd have gone, Your Honor. I'd have given him another mouthful of poison!"

She heard herself, and shuddered. She didn't want to talk like that, and yet that was what she heard herself say. The dreadful words came from her breath, they were formed between her lips. The one who spoke them is not herself, but the Lady who inhabits her body. She is not afraid. If the judge asked her to repeat her words, she would speak them with her own voice, her own breath.

"I'd have liked to see tears in your eyes, but you're a criminal who doesn't weep. However, whether they're dry-eyed or weeping, murderers are condemned to be hanged at the end of a rope."

She is taken to her dungeon cell. Her chains slip along the floor. The sound makes her feel as if she is very tall. The steps of the two guards who follow her are silent. She walks proudly. The sounds of chains is also the distant echo of an ancient sound. They close the door on her. It is cool. Even though outside it is July. She knows so well the constant cold of winter that probes your flesh with needles. In this dungeon cell the cold wriggles across her skin like icy little worms. She knows these walls, which seem to be weeping; she knows the smell of the straw under her blanket; there is nothing in this dungeon cell that she doesn't know. The floor is wood; she would have thought it was stone. She is no longer the little girl who would kneel down at night, elbows resting on a chair, hands joined, piously repeating the invocations that her father addressed to God; she is no longer the little girl bending over her schoolbooks, industriously tracing her letters according to the rigid laws taught her by a nun hidden in a black robe; she is no longer the adolescent who trembled with delight as she put on the dress that her mother had sewn from drawings in an American fashion magazine, and felt her legs turn to jelly when a boy looked at her, blushing, on the street; she is no longer the young girl who, on Mardi Gras, danced late into the night with a soldier; she is no longer the young woman who waited for the return of her husband and the birth of her child, for days as long as weeks and months as long as seasons; she is no longer the young woman with her child in a sleigh laden with sacks and tools who, when she saw the trees open and close like water after a boat has passed, had rested her head on the shoulder of the man who was firmly holding the reins and shouting orders to his horse in a military tone; huddled against Victor, she had loved him as much as his child whom she held in her arms, she had loved him as much as life. She was the woman who had poisoned her man. But that man wasn't Victor, for Victor wouldn't have abandoned a child in the snow: he wouldn't have tossed his child into the storm as he tossed away sacks of provisions and tools, to lighten his burden; he wouldn't have abandoned his child to the beasts of the forest, or the winds. Oh, if that man had been Victor he wouldn't have killed his child! But that man in the storm wasn't Victor, and that woman in the forest wasn't Virginie. In the forest doomed souls wander. They seek bodies like starving beasts. Those souls have invaded their bodies. She was no longer Virginie. He was no longer Victor. It is because of the wind in the trees that everything happened. Everything will go far too quickly now. She will be hanged. Her child will die in her womb. And yet, a boat in a harbor awaited the Lady . . . Never again will she be a young girl who is carried away by dancing, one Mardi Gras night. She knows that, on the Place du Marché, they have started to erect the gibbet where she will be hanged. Pounding hammers, crying saws prepare the gibbet, the platform and the steps that will mount to it. Onlookers will gather to watch her die, to wager on how many times she will cry out before her body stops tossing about at the end of the rope. They will come to comment on the artistry with which the hangman makes the knot around her neck (a little too far to the right, a little too far to the left, too tight, too loose). Someone is taking pains with the construction of her coffin. She does not feel like weeping. If she were Virginie, she would weep. Her inert body will be fastened to the rope, and her soul will drag its chains through the forest's shadows and silence, and through stories told to children on nights when strong winds shake the houses. Then she will be only a Lady without a body, an invisible witness who will convey a small quantity of fear into the light. She cannot prevent life from being what it is: she cannot revive the breathing of that man, she cannot become what she once was: a woman who has not killed.

*   *   *   *   *

The bolt is drawn. That creaking of rusty iron sends shivers down her spine. Is it time for her meal? Time for that greasy soup in an earthen bowl? The door opens. It is not mealtime. Is it the gallows, then? The rope knotted about her neck? She follows the guards. Why are they so fat? Her chains are dragging. Why these chains? She has no desire to run away. She is going, quite simply, toward her end. Why these guards? She walks down corridors that cross. She lets the guards lead her. They move softly. She is going to the gallows. She regrets nothing. Everything that has happened is just. She would prefer not to die. Who can escape death? Her man is dead, the child is dead, she will die and, with her, the seed the man left before he set out for the tree under which he would die. Death is just. No boat awaits the Lady. The knot will tighten about her neck. She is going to die, but she will not forget that stormy night. She will not forget that log cabin in the middle of the forest, where catastrophe abolished speech. She has been here before. She recognizes old photographs of bearded men. Why are their expressions so hard? Henceforth she will encounter only hard expressions. In her last moments she would like to feel some tenderness in the things she will never see again. A door is opened. She has seen this room before, with its windows that give you a view of stone walls. Several men are standing: policemen, guards, men in black robes, monks, men from the forest.

"Do you know this man?"

She recognizes the voice. It is the judge. He repeats his question. She does not know the man who will tie the rope around her neck. The judge insists. She does not want to look. There are too many men in this room. She regrets nothing. It's not easy, when her man is lying lifeless on the ground somewhere, to look at these men who are standing. Nor is it easy for a woman alone to tolerate the looks of all these men.

"Raise your eyes and take a good look."

It is the voice of the judge. He has ordered. She obeys. On the other side of the room, between guards who hold him back, a man with a bearded face attempts to free himself. He resembles that lifeless man in the forest. All at once, the man escapes his guards.

"They don't want me to talk to you, Virginie. Tell them you didn't kill me, Virginie. You can see I'm not dead, Virginie!"

The guards have recaptured the man. They twist his arms behind his back. They choke off his words by pinching his nose. He struggles and groans. More guards arrive. She has let herself be led to a chair. They seat her on it. She remains seated for a long time. Why don't these people go away? All these men around her are too patient. Their expressions are no longer hard. They seem tender. Now they will make her walk to the gallows. Everything will happen much too fast. She is going to die. Her soul will be lost in the wind; her sorrow will hide in the forest spruce. The judge has spoken. She wasn't listening. How can she hear what is said on earth when she is already an old old story, wandering in the wind?

"Do you know this man?"

If he were alive she would know him, but she poisoned him and he fell long ago, under a tree, and the wolves have devoured his remains. A light that is too bright fills the room. The men around her, and further away on the platform, are too white; that man has a blackened face, red eyes, hands wrapped in bandages. She knows that man. She killed him.

"Reply, or you'll be insulting justice and the Court."

There is anger in the judge's voice. Suddenly the bearded man wriggles like a fish and once again he escapes his guards.

"Virginie it's me, it's Victor! You haven't talked for months, but you have to now or those people will hang you by the neck, Virginie, because they say you poisoned me. I know you didn't poison me. But you have to tell them you didn't. You have to talk, Virginie. I love you, Virginie, and I know you didn't poison me. I know I'm not dead. When the other child comes out of your belly you won't be able to keep from crying out. When you cry you'll be crying for me; I won't be far away and I'll come running. Virginie, I'm not dead. Tell them you didn't kill me. They want to hang you because you poisoned me but I can't understand that, I don't want to. I'm alive, Virginie! Listen to me breathe. Tell them I'm alive, Virginie, because they want to hang you. You told them that you poisoned me, Virginie. I ate everything you fixed for me in my sack, and I drank the coffee that you made yourself, and if you'd put poison in the coffee or the food, I'd be face-down on the ground, under a tree. But I'm here, Virginie, and I burned my hands because I'm alive. If I was defunct I wouldn't have got mad at the monks, Virginie, when they told me they'd sent you to the court in the city of Quebec, so you'd be hanged. I'm alive. I'm so full of life I pulled down the monastery; they wanted to have you hanged and now the monks are naked in the woods! I've seen fine forests where the trees spring up like weeds . . . . Virginie, we're going to settle our children around us and that way the good Lord will have to love us. Virginie, be very careful what you say to old monks, because they're a bit deaf; their hearing's bad and besides, monks don't like women. You mustn't go near a monk unless you're with a man . . . . Anyway, I was coming back from the forest, I'd spent more nights there than I expected to, and the cabin door was open but the cabin was empty. You weren't there, there was nothing cooking, no fire in the stove. I looked. You weren't there. I called, I shouted, I started to look in the woods, I shouted, there wasn't a trace of you, Virginie. And since I couldn't ask the birds about you, I decided to go to the monastery. There was nowhere else. They greeted me by throwing holy water at me, as if I was the devil; they sprinkled me as if I was the damned. The monks took off, making signs of the cross, and the men working on the building took up axes or sledgehammers or hammers and started barking like dogs, and all I wanted was to find out if the monks knew where you were. You can see I'm not dead, Virginie, because when they told me you'd been taken to the city of Quebec, to be hanged at the end of a rope in public because you'd poisoned me, well I yelled loud enough for you to hear me, if you were in prison or even if you were already standing in the knot of the rope from the gallows, and I called out your name, Virginie, because I wanted them to know you aren't a murderer, and I called out your name so you'd know I wasn't dead. We had a great misfortune, Virginie, and you shut yourself in silence because you were sad, but you didn't kill me, Virginie, and the good Lord's going to give us another child and you'll forget our catastrophe. I yelled loud enough to frighten the monks and scare them so they'd dirty their soutanes and make them sorry they'd pushed you towards the gallows—monks, who the good Lord put on earth so they'd pass on His forgiveness to sinners. I yelled like I was crazy, Virginie. And then at the same time, some of the men that were working, and the monks, threw themselves at me; and me, I yelled that you hadn't killed me. They caught me, and I ran away, yelling that I wasn't dead and that they wouldn't have you hanged, Virginie. And the first thing I saw was a fire, by the anvil where they were heating iron. I picked up a piece of red-hot iron, I threatened them, I shouted your name, Virginie, and I told them I'd get my revenge because they'd taken you to the gallows, and I threw that red-hot iron on the monastery roof. Even that wasn't enough for my anger, Virginie; with my hands I picked up red-hot coals and I threw them onto the cedar-shingled roof, and then I picked up the embers in my bare hands, like a handful of strawberries, and I threw them in the open window of the chapel, and the roof started smoking right away. Virginie, when the men came back to me my hands were on fire, but I could shout your name, Virginie, and I know that you heard me because you're alive too, Virginie. And life, Virginie, is a fine gift from the Lord. You and me, Virginie, we mustn't refuse the Lord's gift."

"You admit, then, that you set the fire that destroyed the monastery belonging to the community of reverend Trappist monks. Your confession does you honor, but it does not exonerate you."

The judge is speaking. He struggles to keep from yawning.

* * * * *

Outside, the leaves on the maples have turned red, and the frost has started to burn the grass in the fields. The snow came in November. December brought blizzards, icicles hanging from roofs and the hope of spring that seems always more distant: spring, which will free the river of its ice and restore life to everything on earth that is dead. In prison, it is always the same season. The days begin and end, one after the other, the priest announces that it's All Saints' Day or Christmas or Candlemas or Lent. And after mass, the day continues just like yesterday, like many months, like next week. Virginie can feel on the back of her neck that Victor hasn't taken his eyes off her during the service. The rules prohibit them from speaking to one another. At confession Virginie admitted that she had wanted to kill her husband because she was so despondent at having lost her child. The priest asked her if she felt firm regret; she replied that she couldn't regret what she hadn't done, that it wasn't she who had prepared the poison, that it was another soul, not

147

hers, that had wanted to commit the crime and that she could not kill. The priest asked: "How did that come about?" She replied that she didn't know, but that things happen in the forest that are hard to understand. The priest said that he didn't understand. She replied that the good Lord must understand, because it is He who distributes happiness and unhappiness, according to His wishes. The priest added that he would pray for her, for her child and for her husband, and that he wouldn't forget them. And then she was afraid, for priests think only of punishing sin. Her punishment could be only the scaffold, the rope. The judge told her: killing or wanting to kill or intending to kill or trying to kill, all are part of the definition of the same crime. Her belly is very big. A woman came, asked her to lift her skirt, and with big, rough hands she felt Virginie's belly: "That's a child who wants to come out; he won't linger in there." Then all the days seemed alike. Mass on Sunday. The glance exchanged with her husband. He no longer wears bandages on his hands. When he catches sight of her he looks at her, then lowers his head. She has observed that he does the same thing when he passes the tabernacle. That man loves her. As he loves the good Lord. And she wanted to kill him. She bursts into tears. All day, she weeps. The child moves in her belly as if he already wanted to run through the fields. All night she weeps. She hasn't eaten all day. She falls asleep, she dreams that she is weeping, and when she awakens her face is wet with tears. That man loves her. The fat woman with red hands returns; roughly, she feels her belly. "The little one's like his father, he could knock down a wall." Had her husband tried to run away from the prison? "Your man wants to see you; it's not the first door he's knocked down to come and see you." She weeps. But she also feels a smile graze her lips. "By my faith in God, I'll never understand why you listened to the devil when you fixed the poison for that man. Some women don't like to be loved." Some days later, she cries out and they come right away to take her from her cell. The fat woman with callused hands is waiting for her in a room that smells of medicines and burning wood. They have prepared a bed for her. The sheets have been ironed. She weeps again. She doesn't try to stop. Her womb wants to open. It seems to her that the child is crying in her womb. The way her man cried out her name in the forest. The child wants to come out. Her womb is torn. Her belly burns as if it were filled with blazing coals. She cries out her suffering. Someone orders her to push. Her whole body pushes, to cast into life the child that it contains like a kernel. She pushes. Her womb is lacerated and torn. The child is kept back in a prison. She pushes. She pushes like the man who broke down the door of his cell to go and see her. She hurls herself with all her strength, with all her life, with all her pain at what is preventing her child from being born. The flesh tears. It hurts so much. She moans. She cries out the name of her man. She weeps. Now the blazing coals are spread over her whole body. They plead with her to push harder. Gleaming tools, tongs, knives, scissors are set down by her bed. She pushes. The child seems caught in a rope that is tightening about his neck. She weeps. Someone shakes her. Why don't they let her sleep? She hasn't slept for so long. After these nightmares, is she not entitled to keep her eyes closed in her sleep? In the distance a child is crying.

"She's come to!"

She opens her eyes. She sees the fat woman with rough hands. She is holding a swaddled child. It is he who is crying. The fat woman bends over her and lays the child down beside her: once, in the past, a child was presented to her in this way. Is she happy? Is she sad? Through her tears she tries to contemplate the child. Her eyes are veiled by too many tears. At her side, the child grows calm; he doesn't move now as he did in her belly. She feels more happiness than sorrow. She feels a new smile on her lips, but she cannot hold back her tears.

"Monsieur, this is your child, you can come up and look at him, you can touch him: he's yours."

She knows that voice. The judge's voice. But today the voice is no longer threatening.

"My children . . ."

She turns her head. At the foot of her bed the judge is standing with his arms folded on his chest, next to the priest whose arms are folded too.

"My children, God has given you today the gift of the greatest happiness a man and woman can know: that of being a father and mother. The Lord, in His wisdom, wanted to test two children on the path of duty and fidelity. Today, by giving you this child, He is showing you that He forgives you the sins committed in those moments of frenzy that youth often experiences. Am I mistaken, Your Honor?"

The judge shakes his head.

"Accordingly," says the judge, "on the basis of the signs that God has sent us today, and on the basis of the wisdom of the law of Her Britannic Majesty, I declare you both free."

She does not understand the meaning of these flourishes. She hadn't understood him when he sentenced her either.

"Monsieur Your Honor the Judge, does that mean that my wife Virginie and me and the child can go back home, Monsieur le Juge, back to our land, to the cabin I'm going to have to make bigger?"

"Yes, Monsieur, Her Majesty considers that your child has done nothing to warrant prison."

He laughs. The spitefulness that marked his face is now in his laughter. Virginie has caught it. She weeps now as if someone has told her bad news. Her husband dares not approach, but he opens his awkward arms.

"Cry, Virginie, cry. I wish I could cry like you, like a river full of sorrow and joy. But me, I can't cry because I can't believe what's happened to us. We're resurrected, Virginie, like our Lord Jesus Christ: resurrected! But now we have to hurry. We mustn't let the weeds and brushwood get away from us. Hurry, Virginie, we have to go to our land! How I'd love it, Virginie, if we could go to our new world, you and me and the child, on a great ship with sails!"

* * * * *